Edgar A. Smith

On the Marine Mollusca of Ascension Island

Edgar A. Smith

On the Marine Mollusca of Ascension Island

ISBN/EAN: 9783741191022

Manufactured in Europe, USA, Canada, Australia, Japa

Cover: Foto ©Andreas Hilbeck / pixelio.de

Manufactured and distributed by brebook publishing software
(www.brebook.com)

Edgar A. Smith

On the Marine Mollusca of Ascension Island

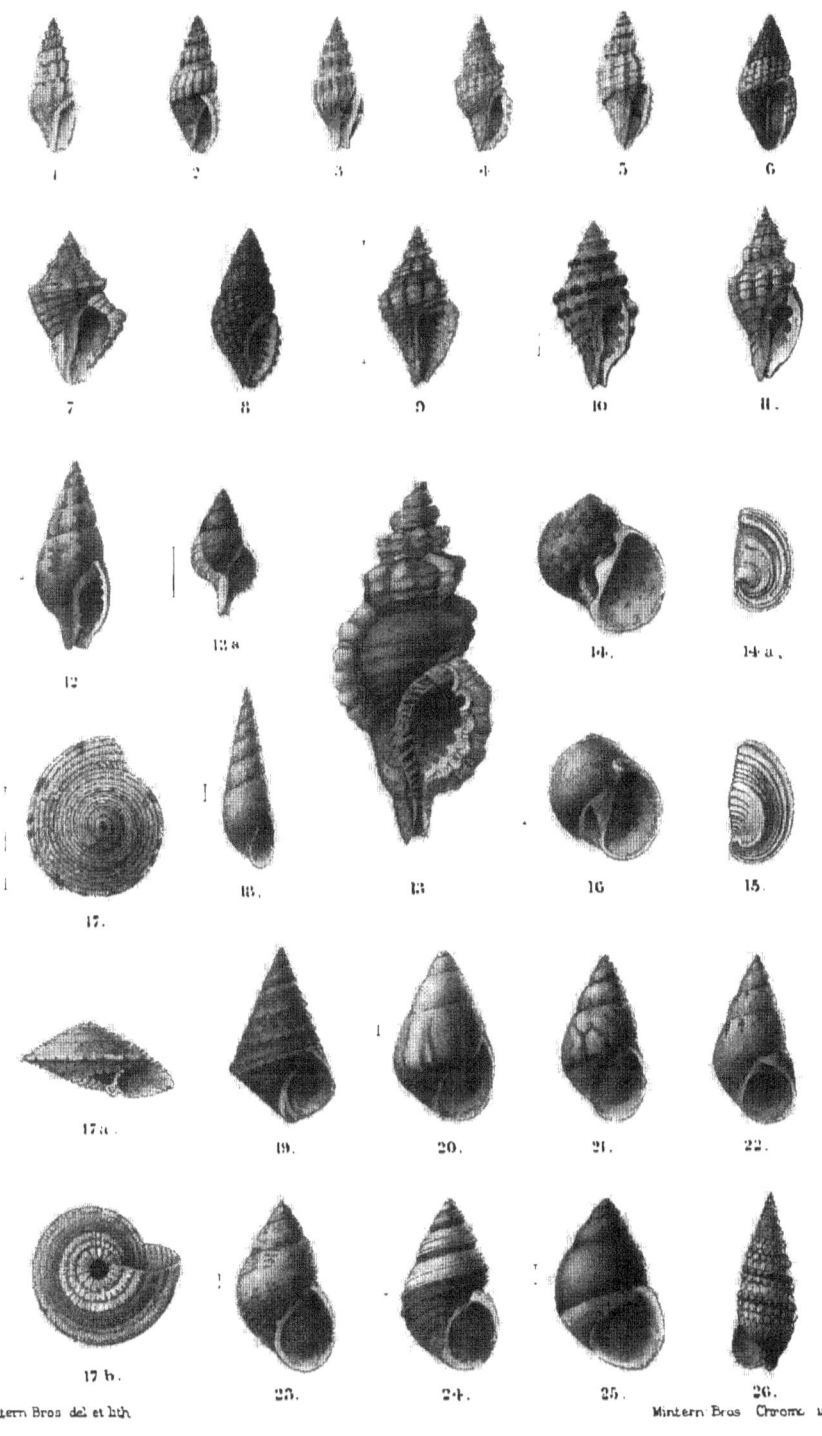

1.   3.   5.   5a   6   7.

4.   8.   2.

8a   9a   8b

9   10a   9b   10

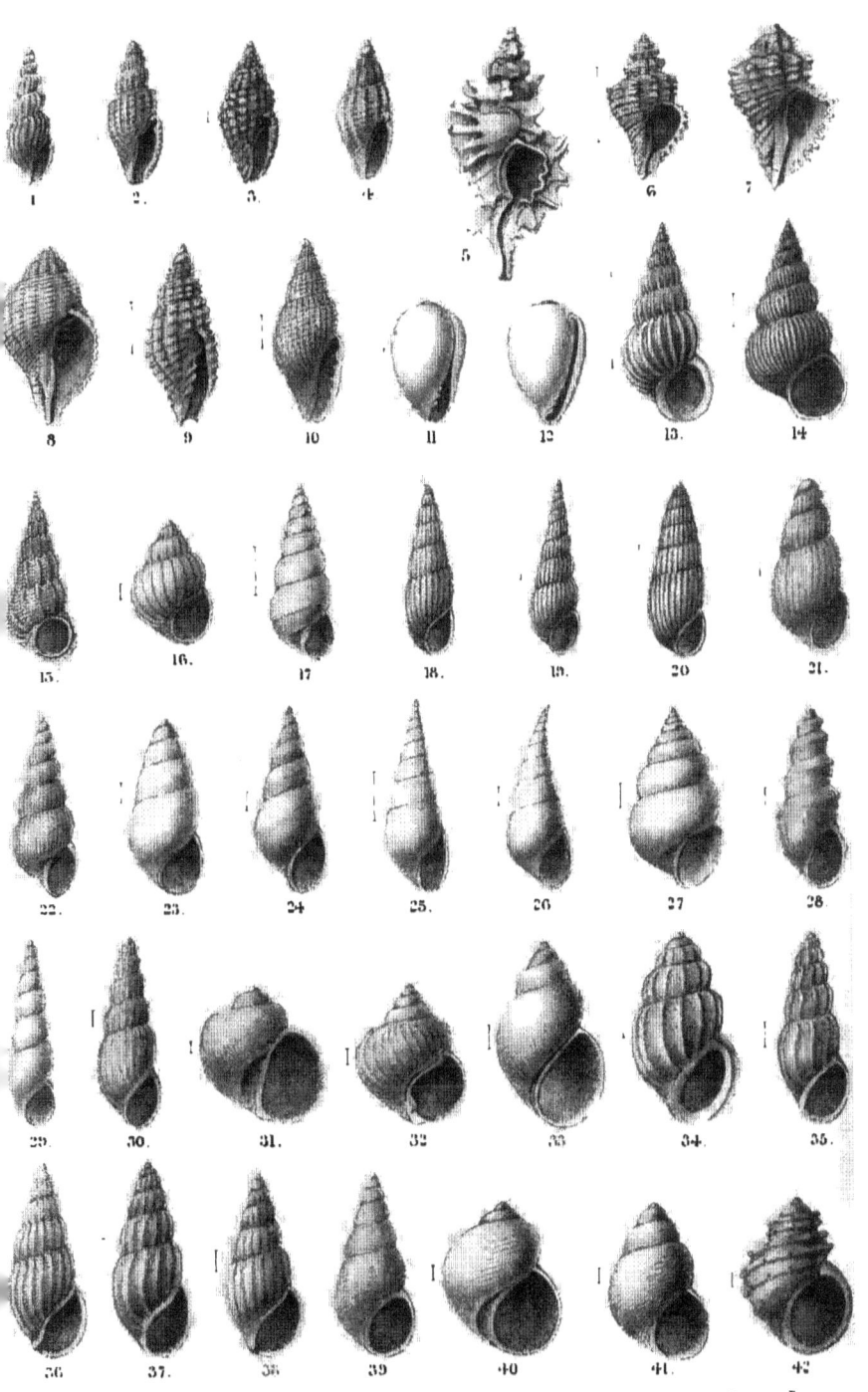

MOLLUSCA OF St HELENA

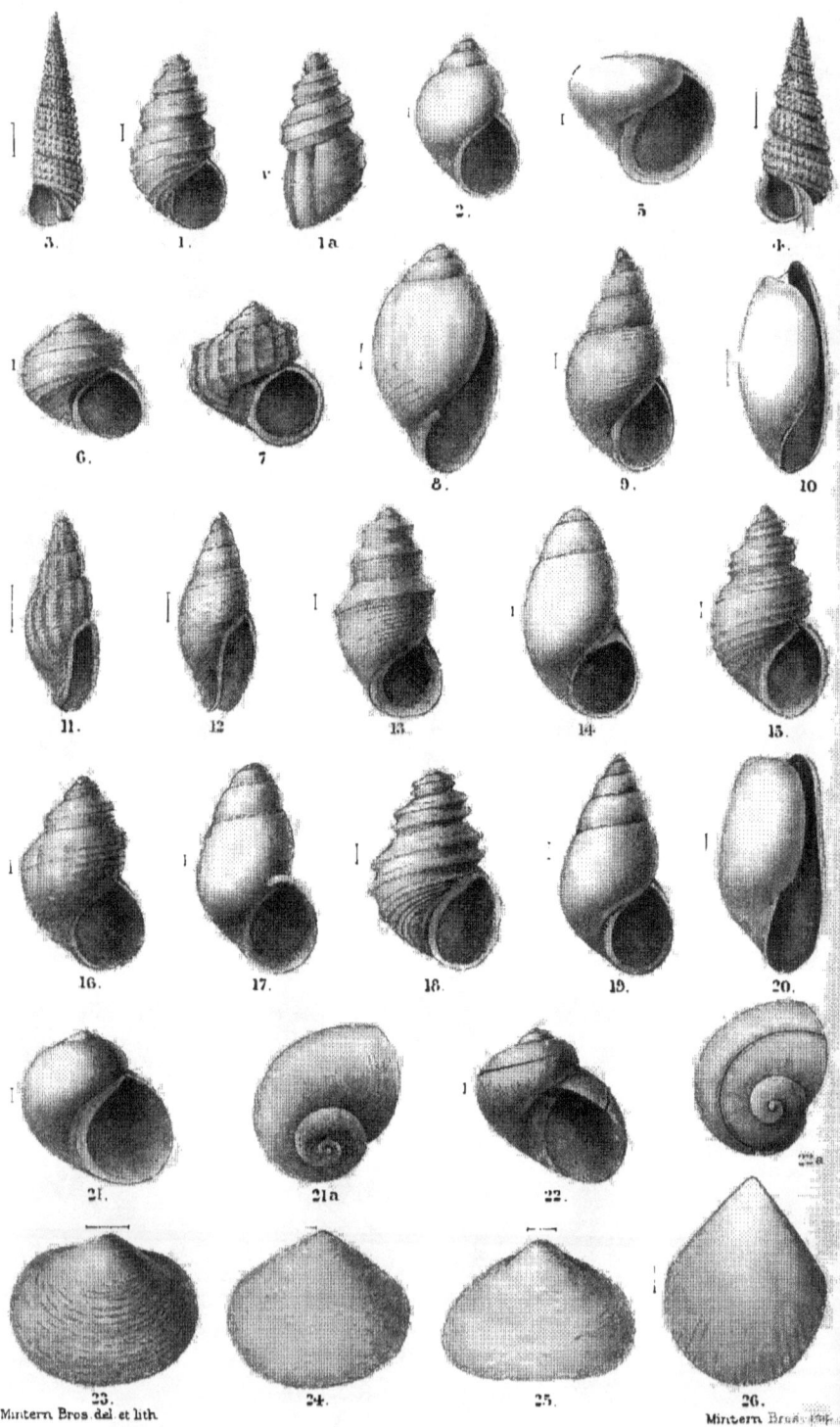

3.

1.

1a.

2.

5.

4.

6.

7.

8.

9.

10

11.

12

13.

14

15.

16.

17.

18.

19.

20.

21.

21a

22.

22a

23.

24.

25.

26.

produce darker cross bands very indistinctly perceptible in certain lights.

Total length 50 inches ; depth of the body behind the head $1\frac{3}{4}$ inch ; depth of the body in the middle of the length $1\frac{1}{2}$ inch ; depth of the body above the vent 7 lines ; length of the head without process 3 inches ; length of the head with the process 5 inches 3 lines ; diameter of the eye 9 lines ; length of the pectoral 10 lines ; length of one of the longest dorsal rays 1 inch 6 lines.

The first figure (Plate XIX.) represents the entire fish, much reduced, with the first dorsal ray restored to its supposed original length and form ; the second figure (Plate XX.) the head of the natural size.

3. Report on the Marine Molluscan Fauna of the Island of St. Helena.   By EDGAR A. SMITH.

[Received March 14, 1890.]

(Plates XXI.–XXIV.)

The materials which form the basis of this Report consist mainly of a very extensive series of shells, about 2500 in number, collected at St. Helena by Capt. W. H. Turton, R.E., during the years 1884–6, and which he subsequently most liberally presented to the British Museum.

A series of small shells, presented to the Museum in 1857 by E. W. Alexander, Esq., has also been worked through. A few specimens dredged by Dr. Wallich about the year 1857, others received from Sir George Grey in 1841, a small collection from the Museum of Economic Geology in 1860, and, finally, a set of the specimens collected by Mr. J. C. Melliss and enumerated in his book on St. Helena, have been examined.

The greatest praise is due to Capt. Turton for the excellent manner in which the collection was made and put up for transmission to this country ; and the amount of time and labour bestowed upon it must have been very considerable.

The majority of the species are very small and were obtained " by sifting the sand and shingle which is found in a few places on the coast," and by dredging in depths up to about 80 fathoms, chiefly, but not exclusively, off the north of the island. A few were picked out of a hard kind of conglomerate of shells and sand, about four feet above high-water mark, in a bay on the north coast. This conglomerate is found in the crevices of rocks which have fallen down from the high cliffs above, quite recently, and probably it got washed up into that position by some high tide, such as occurs there every few years. Some of the specimens were found on pieces of a substance, locally called " Sea-horn " [1], which is sometimes

---

[1] Doubtless these pieces of " Sea-horn " are portions of a large species of Tangle, probably *Ecklonia buccinalis*, which is very thick and horny, and occurs at the Cape of Good Hope, whence these fragments had drifted.

washed ashore on the windward or south side of the island. These specimens will be enumerated in an Appendix, as they cannot be regarded as belonging to the St. Helena fauna. In nearly every instance in which it has been possible to associate them with known species, they prove to be South-African forms, thus clearly showing that they have been drifted northwards from the Cape by the prevailing south-east trade-winds and oceanic currents.

Capt. Turton observes in his notes that some of them were alive when taken, and this was generally the case when the "Sea-horn" was only recently washed up, or was secured from a boat. Notwithstanding this fact, it is remarkable that scarcely any (*exclusively*) South-African species appear to survive and become established at St. Helena; indeed, *Gadinia costata* is the only species in this collection, not found on "Sea-horn," the distribution of which has hitherto been restricted to South Africa. A few species such as *Triton olearium, Triforis perversa, Cingulina circinata, Saxicava arctica, Mytilus edulis, M. magellanicus, Arca domingensis, Pinna pernula,* and perhaps one or two others, are found at both localities, but they mostly have a wide distribution.

As it is seen that many species are drifted from the Cape to St. Helena, the question arises whether some of those dredged by Capt. Turton, or found by him and others upon the shore, may not have become detached from the floating seaweed.

In one or two cases it is pretty certain that this has occurred, as specimens of *Mytilus magellanicus* and *M. edulis* (?) were obtained alive attached to floating weed and also dead upon the shore. Two dead specimens of *Patella compressa*, a well-known Cape species, were also collected on the shore, there being every probability of their having been carried there attached to seaweed.

The molluscan fauna of St. Helena appears most to resemble that of the West Indies; for, of the known species[1] in this collection, just fifty per cent. are common to the two localities.

About five-and-twenty species, or thirty per cent., are identical with Mediterranean forms, and about half a dozen occur at all three localities. About thirteen species are also met with on the West-African Coast, between the Gulf of Guinea and Morocco.

What proportion of species are common to St. Helena and the west coast of Africa, south of Guinea, it is difficult to ascertain at present, as comparatively little is known of the Mollusca of that part of the coast.

However, in Dunker's list of shells from Lower Guinea, eight species are quoted which are common to St. Helena. The similarity between the fauna of St. Helena and that of the West Indies is undoubtedly, in a great measure, due to oceanic currents.

According to various maps an important current flows from near the centre of the South Atlantic past Ascension Island along the north coast of South America to the West Indies, a return current passing in an easterly or south-easterly direction towards the Gulf of Guinea. These and the great Gulf-stream in all probability have

[1] Pelagic forms are not included.

tended to assimilate, to some extent, the faunas of the West Indies and West Africa by transmitting from place to place the pelagic fry of some of the species, and the adult forms and the ova of others attached to floating sea weed.

Not more than fourteen species in this collection belong to forms which occur in the Indo-Pacific region. This comparative paucity of species common to these two regions is probably, in a great measure, attributable to the cold Antarctic currents, which, flowing northward to the Cape of Good Hope, bar the emigration of species from the Indian Ocean into the Atlantic. Semper[1] refers to the sudden and marked change in the fauna on rounding the Cape, the result of different currents and temperature.

The only list of species from St. Helena which has yet appeared is that prepared by Jeffreys[2], which was based upon a collection made by Mr. Melliss, who, in his book on St. Helena (pp. 113–128), has reproduced and somewhat amplified it. In this list only forty-one marine species are enumerated, the majority consisting of shells of fairly large dimensions, which, with one exception (*Ostrea crista-galli*), were all picked up on the shore.

This list did not contain all the species which had been previously recorded from the island, at least half a dozen forms being omitted.

The large proportion of new species hereafter described, most of them very small, is not therefore altogether surprising, as so little was previously known of this fauna.

Thanks to Capt. Turton's energy, as many as 138 additional named species are now added to the list, bringing up the total of known forms to 178.

This number, however, does not at all approximate the total of the species which really exist around St. Helena; for, in addition to those which I have been able to determine, there is a considerable number, nearly a hundred species, which, on account of their immature or bad condition, could not be satisfactorily identified or described. Besides, whenever more extensive dredging is carried on, many additional species will doubtless be discovered[3].

A certain number of species have been described from St. Helena which in reality do not inhabit that region. This mistake has arisen from the misspelling of St. Elena on the west coast of America. The species are :—(1) *Cancellaria tessellata*, Sowerby ; (2) *C. obtusa*, Kiener (non Deshayes)=*C. solida*, Sow. ; (3) *Marginella granum*, Kiener=*Erato scabriuscula*, Gray ; (4) *Purpura undata*, Lamarck, partim =*P. biserialis*, Blainv.; (5) *Ostrea columbiensis*, Hanley ; (6) *Circe fluctuata*, Sow.; (7) *Strombus granulatus*, Gray[4].

---

[1] Animal Life, p. 278.   [2] Ann. Mag. Nat. Hist. 1872, vol. ix. pp. 262–4.
[3] Specimens of *Cypræa testudinaria, C. moneta, C. arabica,* and *Placuna sella* were obtained by Capt. Turton as St. Helena shells ; but he shrewdly doubted their genuineness. He observes, "ships from all parts of the world touch here, often bringing shells which are got by the natives, and then offered as island shells." This is evidently the true explanation of the presence of these species at St. Helena.
[4] Species 1 to 4 are quoted from Kiener's 'Icon. Coq. Viv.,' and 5, 6, and 7 from Reeve's 'Conch. Icon.'

Purpura turbinoides, Blainville, quoted by Kiener from St. Helena, occurs at the Phillipine Islands and in the Pacific.

The following Table will show at a glance the distribution of each species, which, in some instances, is very remarkable. Doubtless many of the new species, which are indicated by an asterisk *, will eventually be discovered in other localities.

TABLE OF DISTRIBUTION.

Complete List of known Species.	WEST ATLANTIC.			EAST ATLANTIC.									Localities, chiefly Extra-Atlantic.
	W. Indies.	Fernando Noronha.	Brazil.	S. Africa.	St. Helena.	Ascension.	W. Africa.	Cape Verde I.	Canary I.	Azores.	Mediterranean.	British.	
Conus testudinarius					*		*	*					E. coast of South and [Central America [(*Weinkauff*).
—— sp.					*								
—— irregularis					*		*						
Pleurotoma (Clavus) amanda					*								
* —— (——) prolongata					*								
* —— (——) albobalteata					*								
* —— (Drillia) turtoni					*								
—— (Mangilia) subquadrata					*								
—— (——) gemma					*								
* —— (——) mellissi					*								
* —— (Clathurella ?) commutabilis					*								
* —— (——) multigranosa					*								
* —— (——) usta					*								
Murex (Chicoreus) adustus	*				*								Japan, Philippines, [Indian and Pacific [Oceans.
* —— (Ocinebra) sanctæ-helenæ					*								
* —— (——) patruelis					*								
* —— (——) alboangulatus					*								
* Lachesis helenæ					*								
* Cantharus (Tritonidea) albozonatus					*								
* —— (——) consanguineus					*								
* —— (——) lævis					*								
Columbella (Anachis) decipiens	*				*								
—— (Mitrella) cribraria	*				*	*	*						Java, Panama, Ma-[zatlan.
—— (——) pusilla	*				*								
* —— (——) sanctæ-helenæ					*								
Nassa sanctæ-helenæ					*								
—— cinctella					*								
* Coralliophila erythrostoma					*								
* —— atlantica					*								
—— bracteata					*						*		
Purpura helena	*				*	*	*						
* Mitra (Cancilla) turtoni					*								
* —— (Turricula) innotabilis					*								
* —— (Pusia) sanctæ-helenæ					*								
* —— (Thala) pleurotomoides					*								
Marginella (Volvaria) cinerea					*								
* —— (——) consanguinea					*								
* —— (——) atomus					*								

TABLE (*continued*).

Complete List of known Species.	West Atlantic.			East Atlantic.									Localities, chiefly Extra-Atlantic.
	W. Indies.	Fernando Noronha.	Brazil.	S. Africa.	St. Helena.	Ascension.	W. Africa.	Cape Verde I.	Canary I.	Azores.	Mediterranean.	British.	
Cassis testiculus	*	...	...	...	*	...	*						
Triton tritonis	*	...	...	...	*			*	*	...	*	...	N. Australia, Pacific I.
—— olearium	*	...	*	*	*						*	...	Australia, Japan, &c.
* —— turtoni	...	...	...	...	*								
Ranella cœlata	...	...	...	...	*	*	*	...	...	...	...	...	Panama.
—— thomæ	*	...	...	...	*			*	*	...	...		Mauritius.
* Natica turtoni	...	...	...	...	*								
—— dillwynii	*	...	...	...	*				...	...	*	...	Mauritius, S. Pacific I.
* —— sanctæ-helenæ	...	...	...	...	*								
—— (Polinices) porcellana	...	...	...	...	*			*	*				
Ianthina communis													⎫
—— globosa (*fide Lesson*)													⎪ Pelagic forms
—— pallida													⎬ throughout the
—— umbilicata													⎪ Atlantic.
—— exigua													⎭
Scalaria confusa	...	...	...	...	*								Philippines, Sandwich
—— fragilis	*	...	...	...	*								[I., N.W. Australia.
* —— mellissi	...	...	...	...	*								
* —— sanctæ-helenæ	...	...	...	...	*								
* —— commoda	...	...	...	...	*								
* —— atomus	...	...	...	...	*								
* —— multistriata ?	*	...	...	...	*?	...	...	...					
Obeliscus dolabratus	*	...	...	...	*	...	*	...	...	...	...	...	Red Sea, Indian and
* —— sanctæ-helenæ	...	...	...	...	*								[Pacific Oceans.
* —— (Syrnola) pumilio	...	...	...	...	*								
* Turbonilla haroldi	...	...	...	...	*								
* —— assimilans	...	...	...	...	*								
* —— truncatelloides	...	...	...	...	*								
* —— brachia	...	...	...	...	*								
* —— eritima	...	...	...	...	*								
Cingulina circinata	...	...	...	*	*	...	...	...	...	...	...	...	N. China, Japan, Port
—— (Mathilda) quadricarinata	...	...	...	...	*	...	...	...	*	...	*		[Jackson.
* Odostomia glaphyra	...	...	...	...	*								
* Eulima fuscescens	...	...	...	...	*								
* —— atlantica	...	...	...	...	*								
—— subconica	...	...	...	...	*								
* —— germana	...	...	...	...	*								
* —— (Subularia) fuscopunctata	...	...	...	...	*								
* Amaurella canaliculata	...	...	...	...	*								
Cioniscus unicus	...	...	...	...	*						*	*	
* Aclis angulata	...	...	...	...	*								
* —— simillima	...	...	...	...	*								
* —— didyma	...	...	...	...	*								
Solarium placentale	...	*	...	...	*								California.
* —— ordinarium	...	...	...	...	*								
—— hybridum	...	...	...	...	*						*	...	Indian Ocean, Japan.
—— architæ	...	...	...	...	*	...	...	...			*		[Philippines, E.
Cypræa lurida	...	...	...	...	*	*	*	*	*	*	*		[Australia, &c.

TABLE (continued).

Complete List of known Species	West Atlantic			East Atlantic									Localities, chiefly Extra-Atlantic.
	W. Indies.	Fernando Noronha.	Brazil.	S. Africa.	St. Helena.	Ascension.	W. Africa.	Cape Verde I.	Canary I.	Azores.	Mediterranean.	British.	
Cypraea spurca	*	...	...	...	*	*	*	*	*	*	*	...	Mauritius.
Littorina miliaris	...	...	...	...	*	*							
* —— helenae	...	...	...	...	*								
Modulus modulus	*	...	...	...	*								
Planaxis lineatus	*	...	...	...	*	*							
—— eboreus	*	...	...	...	*								
* Lacuna pumilio	...	...	...	...	*								
Fossarus ambiguus	...	...	...	...	*	...	*	*	*	*	*		
* —— (Couthouyia) dentifer	...	...	...	...	*								
* —— (——) laeviusculus	...	...	...	...	*								
* Diala fuscopicta	...	...	...	...	*								
* Rissoina mellissii	...	...	.	...	*								
* —— turtoni	...	...	...	...	*								
* —— decipiens	...	...	...	...	*								
—— bryeria	*	...	...	...	*	*	...	...	...	...	...	...	Mauritius.
* —— congenita	...	...	...	...	*								
* —— helenae	...	...	...	...	*								
* Rissoa cala	...	...	...	...	*								
* —— ephamilla	...	...	...	...	*								
* —— glypta	...	...	...	...	*								
* —— critima	...	...	...	...	*								
* —— agapeta	...	...	...	...	*								
* —— compsa	...	...	...	...	*								
* —— wallichi	...	...	...	...	*								
* —— perfecta	...	...	...	...	*								
* —— varicifera	...	...	...	...	*								
* —— pseustes	...	...	...	...	*								
* Barleeia congenita	...	...	...	...	*								
Caecum jucundum	*	...	...	...	*								
—— imbricatum	*	...	...	...	*								
—— (Meioceras) nitidum	*	...	...	...	*								
Cerithium (Bittium) gibberulum	*	...	...	...	*								
Triforis perversa	...	...	...	*	*	...	*	...	*	*	*	*	California.
—— melanura	*	...	...	...	*								
* —— atlantica	...	...	...	...	*								
* —— recta	...	...	...	...	*								
* —— bathyraphe	...	...	...	...	*								
Cirithiopsis rugulosa	*	...	...	...	*								
—— neglecta	...	...	...	...	*	...	...	...	...	...	...	...	Panama.
Hipponyx antiquatus	*	*	...	...	*	*	*						
—— grayanus		*	...	...	*	...	...	...	...	...	...	...	W. coast of C. America
* Teinostoma ? abnorme	...	...	...	...	*								[and Sandwich I.
Turbo (Collonia) rubricinctus	...	...	...	...	*	...	...	...	...	...	...	...	Sandwich I.
* —— (——) admissus	...	...	...	...	*								
Phasianella tessellata	*	...	...	...	*								
* Liotia arenula	...	...	...	...	*								
* —— admirabilis	...	...	...	...	*								
Gena asperulata	*	...	...	...	*								
Emarginula elongata	...	...	...	...	*	...	...	...	...	...	...	*	

TABLE (continued).

Complete List of known Species.	W. Indies	Fernando Noronha	Brazil	S. Africa	St. Helena	Ascension	W. Africa	Cape Verde I.	Canary I.	Azores	Mediterranean	British	Localities, chiefly Extra-Atlantic.
Fissurella gibberula?					*		*		*		*		Spain, Portugal.
Patella plumbea					*		*						
Williamia gussonii					*	*			*	*	*		Sandwich I.
Bulla striata	*		*		*		*			*	*		
Cylichna cylindracea			*		*	*	*				*	*	
* —— atlantica					*								
—— bidentata	*				*								
Tornatina recta	*				*								
Philine quadrata					*					*		*	Massachusetts Bay,
Haminea hydatis					*	*					*	*	[Greenland.
* Actæon semisculptus					*?								
* Leucotina minuta					*								
Umbrella mediterranea?				*?	*?		*				*		
Tylodina citrina									*	*	*		
Pedipes afer					*		*				*		Madeira.
Gadinia costata				*	*								
Cadulus jeffreysii					*		*			*	*	*	New England.
Venus (Ventricola) effossa					*		*			*	*		
—— (Chione) pygmæa	*				*								
Cytherea (Caryatis) rudis					*					*			
Tellina antonii	*				*								
Semele cordiformis	*		*		*		*						West Colombia.
Ervilia subcancellata	*	*	*		*								
Corbula swiftiana	*				*								
Cardium (Fragum) speciosum					*								China Sea.
—— (Papyridea) bullatum	*		*		*					*			W. coast of C. America.
Rocellaria dubia					*			*	*		*	*	Madeira.
Chama sp.					*								
—— gryphoides (fide Jeffreys)					*				*		*		
* Basterotia oblonga					*								
Lasæa adansoniana					*		*						
* Lucina inconspicua					*								
* —— (Codakia) compacta					*								
Verticordia ornata	*				*								California, China Sea,
Mytilus exustus	*	*	*		*								[United States.
Lithodomus biexcavatus?	*				*?								
* Arca sanctæ-helenæ					*	*							
—— (Acar) domingensis	*			*	*	*		*					Red Sea, Japan, Australia, Indian and Pacific Oceans.
Pinna rugosa					*?								? Bay of Panama.
—— pernula	*			*	*								Madeira.
Avicula hirundo (fide Jeffreys)					*					*	*	*	
Pecten corallinoides					*			*	*	*			
* —— atlanticus					*								
* —— (Janira) turtoni					*								[tugal.
Limea sarsii					*					*	*		W. of Ireland to Por-
Ostrea crista-galli (fide Jeffreys)					*								Indian Ocean.
—— sp.					*								

I. CEPHALOPODA.

An undetermined species of *Octopus* and the shells of *Argonauta argo* are mentioned by Mr. Melliss. The former "is plentiful in the nooks and rocky holes on the coast, about high-water mark." The *Argonauta* is occasionally washed ashore at Sandy Bay, on the south coast; this species also occurs at the Cape, in the Mediterranean, North Atlantic, Indian and Pacific Oceans.

II. PTEROPODA.

Shells of the following species[1] were dredged in 50 to 80 fathoms :—

1. CAVOLINIA TRIDENTATA (Forskål).

2. CAVOLINIA LONGIROSTRIS (Lesueur).

3. CAVOLINIA QUADRIDENTATA (Lesueur).

4. CAVOLINIA UNCINATA (Rang).

5. CAVOLINIA GIBBOSA (Rang).

6. CAVOLINIA INFLEXA (Lesueur).

7. DIACRIA TRISPINOSA (Lesueur).

8. CLIO PYRAMIDATA, Linné.

9. STYLIOLA SUBULA, Quoy & Gaimard.

10. STYLIOLA RECTA, Lesueur.

11. STYLIOLA VIRGATA, Rang.

12. TRIPTERA COLUMELLA, Rang.

13. LIMACINA BULIMOIDES, D'Orbigny.

14. LIMACINA INFLATA, D'Orbigny.

15. LIMACINA ANTARCTICA, Woodward.

III. GASTROPODA.

CONUS TESTUDINARIUS, Martini.

Two specimens were obtained by Mr. Melliss.

CONUS IRREGULARIS, Sowerby.

The specimens from St. Helena are of a shorter growth than those figured by Sowerby (Thes. Conch. iii. pl. 104. figs. 418, 419); they are broader at the shoulder and more suddenly contracted anteriorly. They also are more highly painted, exhibiting a considerable amount of olive-brown longitudinal streaks, which are interrupted at the

[1] For the synonymy and distribution consult Pelseneer's Report on the Pteropoda of the 'Challenger' Expedition.

middle by the bluish-white irregular zone dotted and spotted with olive-brown. The spire is either almost uniformly dark chestnut-brown, or else white, blotched with that colour.

Some small specimens, about ¾ inch long, which I believe to be the young of this species, are still more brightly coloured, being more or less copiously blotched with brown-black ; and the spire is radiately lined and spotted with the same tint.

CONUS sp. ?

A single much-worn shell is all that was obtained. In general form it is very like *C. tiniunus*, but seems to be thicker and more strongly striated transversely. It is livid in colour, and marked with longitudinal and transverse bands of an olive-brown tint, which are not, however, sharply defined, but blend at the edges into the ground-colour of the shell. The whorls of the spire are dark livid on the upper half and pale beneath, forming a light spiral zone which revolves up the spire above the suture.

PLEUROTOMA (CLAVUS) AMANDA, Smith. (Plate XXI. fig. 1.)

Pleurotoma (Clavus) amanda, Smith, Ann. & Mag. Nat. Hist. Sept. 1882, p. 207.

The locality of this species was unknown at the time it was described. The fresh specimens from St. Helena have the transverse zone of a brighter tint, somewhat pinkish red. In certain examples it is interrupted between the ribs, and occasionally a fine reddish line occurs at the upper part of the whorls a little below the suture.

This species is very closely related to *P. sinuosa*, Montagu, and may eventually prove to be merely a variety of it.

PLEUROTOMA (CLAVUS) PROLONGATA. (Plate XXIII. fig. 1.)

Testa elongata, turrita, alba vel rubescens ; anfractus 6–7, duo apicales læves, magni, globosi, sequentes superne vix concave declives, in medio angulati, inferne conspicue contracti, costis obliquis flexuosis circa 12 instructi ; apertura parva, brevis, longit. totius ⅓ adæquans ; anfr. ultimus costa valida variciformi longe pone labrum munitus ; labrum tenue, haud incrassatum ; sinus profundus, magnus ; columella rectiuscula, callo tenui labro juncta ; canalis brevissimus, latus.

Longit. 6 millim., diam. 2.

This species is remarkable for the great length of the spire in proportion to that of the aperture. Besides the ribs, the surface exhibits fine wavy striæ of growth.

PLEUROTOMA (CLAVUS) ALBOBALTEATA. (Plate XXI. fig. 2.)

Testa parva, fusiformi-ovata, pallide fuscescens, circa medium anfr. superiorum et ad basim anfr. ultimi albida ; anfr. 6, primi duo læves, convexi, cæteri paulo excavati, ad latera convexiusculi, costis crassis 10–12 superne subobsoletis, ad suturas indistincte

18*

subnodosis (in anfr. ult. infr. medium evanidis) instructi ; apertura parva, longit. totius ½ haud æquans; labrum ad marginem tenue, costa ultima valida extus incrassatum, superne leviter sinuatum.

Longit. 5 *millim., diam.* 2.

Although the general appearance of this little species as regards colour is as above described, still, on closer examination, the style of ornamentation proves to be less simple ; the white band is seen to be subdivided by a fine line of the same colour as the rest of the shell, and a few wavy darker brown lines flow down the lower portion of the body-whorl.

One specimen has the brown colour replaced by a pinkish or vinous tint.

PLEUROTOMA (DRILLIA) TURTONI.   (Plate XXI. fig. 3.)

Testa breviter fusiformis, flavescens, inter costas fusco tincta, infra suturas alba, circa anfr. ultimi medium albo zonata ; anfr. 10½, *primus convexus, lævis, duo sequentes in medio carinati, cæteri superne concavi, deinde convexi, costis brevibus circiter* 12 *superne obsoletis lirisque spiralibus* 4–6 *inter costas fuscis decussati, infra suturam corrugati ; anfr. ultimus inferne contractus ; apertura angusta, longit. totius ½ paulo minor ; labrum ad marginem tenue, extus costa variciforme arcuata incrassatum, intus denticulatum ; columella alba, denticulis transversis pluribus munita ; sinus profundus ; canalis brevis, recurvus.*

Longit. 18 *millim., diam.* 6.

The colouring of this species is very pretty. The spire has the appearance of being alternately zoned with white and yellow, the yellow zone, falling upon the lower and costate portion of the whorls, is interrupted by a brown stain between the ribs. The lower half of the body-whorl, excepting the pale extremity, is yellowish, and has the appearance of being dotted with brown.

This species belongs to that section of the genus which includes *Pl. intercalaris,* Carpenter, *Pl. spurca,* Hinds, and a few others. These species have the columella and the interior of the labrum more or less denticulated.

PLEUROTOMA (MANGILIA) SUBQUADRATA, Smith.   (Plate XXI. fig. 4.)

This species was described in the Ann. & Mag. Nat. Hist. 1888, vol. ii. p. 313.

PLEUROTOMA (MANGILIA) GEMMA, Smith.   (Plate XXIII. fig. 2.)

Pleurotoma (Mangilia) gemma, Smith, Ann. & Mag. Nat. Hist. 1884, xiv. p. 322.

The specimens obtained by Mr. Turton are larger and in fresher condition than those originally described, and show that the upper ends of the costæ are not constantly red alternately, as some of these examples have all of them of a reddish colour. The largest specimen has eight whorls, of which the three apical are white, convex, and ornamented with subdistant, very oblique, arcuate, and very slender liræ. The remainder of the shell is of a whitish-wax tint. The length is 7⅔ millim., the diameter 3.

The more extended series of specimens at hand now shows that *Pl. helenensis*, which I described at the same time as *Pl. gemma*, is only a variety of this species, differing chiefly from the typical form in colour.

Some examples are entirely white, others of a uniform rich brown, whilst others are of intermediate tints. Some have all the upper ends of the costæ of a reddish colour, some only the alternate ones; and the transverse zone on the body-whorl is not constantly present in all specimens; indeed it appears to be mostly wanting in the yellowish and brownish examples. *Pl. lavalleana*, d'Orbigny, is the West-Indian representative of this species, from which it differs in the position of the colour-band, its more attenuated body-whorl, and in the different position of the angle of the volutions.

PLEUROTOMA (MANGILIA) MELLISSI.   (Plate XXI. fig. 5.)

Testa parva, fusiformi-ovata, dilute fuscescens ad suturas fusco tincta, circa medium anfr. ultimi fusco zonata; anfractus 6½, primi 2½ convexi, læves, tertius convexus, obliquiter tenuissime liratus, cæteri superne declives et angulati, costis tenuibus circa 14 et liris gracilioribus spiralibus (in anfr. superioribus 3, in ultimo 16–20) cancellati, undique minute squamoso-striati; apertura angusta, longit. totius ½ vix æquans; labrum incrassatum, intus læve; sinus haud profundus.

Longit. 5 *millim., diam.* 2.

The microscopic structure of this species is very like that occurring in *Pl. subquadrata*, and appears under the microscope to consist of numerous spiral series of very minute grain-like scales, which, at times, are arranged one under the other, so as to produce the appearance of longitudinal series also. It may be known from *Pl. subquadrata* by its finer cancellation and the more central position of the colour-zone upon the body-whorl, which also is not contracted in the same way below the middle.

PLEUROTOMA (CLATHURELLA ?) COMMUTABILIS.   (Plate XXIII. fig. 3.)

Testa parva, fusiformi-ovata, aut alba, flavescens, aut lilacea, costis longitudinalibus ad 12 lirisque transversis (in anfr. superioribus 2–3, in ultimo 8), fortissime cancellata; anfractus 5½, primi 1½ vitrei, peculiares, superne carinati et concavi, quasi truncati, reliqui 4 convexiusculi; apertura parva, angusta, longit. totius ⅜ adæquans; labrum vix incrassatum; canalis brevissimus, latus; sinus parvus, inconspicuus; columella rectiuscula, tuberculis duobus prope medium munita.

Longit. 4 *millim., diam.* 1½.

This species is very distinctly characterized by its form and the coarse style of its sculpture. The ribs and liræ are about equally thick, produced into acute nodules at the points of intersection, and the quadrate interstices are very deeply pitted.

PLEUROTOMA (CLATHURELLA?) MULTIGRANOSA. (Plate XXI. fig. 6.)

Testa parva, fusiformi-ovata, nigrescens vel rufescens, supra medium anfractuum albo zonata, undique granulis albis et nigrescentibus aut rufis ornata ; anfractus 5½, nucleares 1½ læves, cornei, superne concavi, carinati, cæteri planiusculi, costis ad 14 lirisque spiralibus supra costas granosis instructi ; liræ in anfr. superioribus tres, suprema minima, in ultimo 13–14 ; apertura angusta, longit. totius ½ subæquans ; columella rectiuscula, in medio tuberculis minutis duobus instructa, callo tenui induta ; labrum vix incrassatum, superne brevissime sed distincte sinuatum.

Longit. 4¼ *millim., diam.* 2.

This species is larger than *Pl. commutabilis,* differently coloured, and more closely sculptured. The costæ and liræ are so near together that the granules almost touch one another.

PLEUROTOMA (CLATHURELLA?) USTA. (Plate XXIII. fig. 4.)

Testa minuta, fusiformi-ovata, nigricans vel rufescens, interdum serie granulorum albidorum paulo infra suturam ornata ; anfract. 5, primi 1½ lævigati, cæteri leviter convexiusculi, costis 12–14 paulo obliquis instructi, sulcisque angustis transversis (in anfr. superioribus 4, in ultimo circiter 15) sculpti ; apertura elongata, angusta, dimidium longit. totius vix æquans ; columella leviter obliqua, callo tenui induta, in medio interdum indistincte incisa ; labrum probabiliter leviter incrassatum, superne vix sinuatum.

Longit. 2¾ *millim., diam.* 1½.

The sulci cut through the costæ and produce a somewhat granular appearance. The lira beneath the first sulcus below the suture is that which is white upon the riblets in the black variety.

MUREX (CHICOREUS) ADUSTUS, Lamarck.

Hab. West Indies, Japan, Philippines, Indian and Pacific Oceans.

In the 'Annals and Magazine of Natural History,' 1875, vol. xv. p. 419, I expressed an opinion that *Murex despectus* of A. Adams, said to have come from the West Indies, was identical with this species, which is known as an inhabitant of Eastern seas. At the time I doubted the accuracy of the locality given by Adams, but now I am inclined to believe it correct, as so many West-Indian shells have also been found on the eastern side of the Atlantic at St. Helena, Ascension Island, and on the west coast of Africa.

MUREX (OCINEBRA) SANCTÆ-HELENÆ. (Plate XXIII. fig. 5.)

Testa fusiformis, alba, varicibus tribus obliquis, compressis, dentatis, et liris spiralibus (in anfract. superioribus duobus, in ultimo

5–6) *pone varices maxime elevatis instructa; anfractus circa* 10, *superne concavi, dein angulati, inferne constricti; apertura parva, irregulariter circularis, marginibus fere continuis prominentibus circumdata; canalis mediocriter elongatus, angustus, subclausus, tortuosus, recurvus.*

Longit. 30 *millim., lat.* 16.

This species is remarkable for the prominent character of the spiral ridges just behind the varices and the deep pits between them. They are produced in a somewhat radiating manner, and form tooth-like projections, giving the edge of the varices a pretty festooned appearance. Although four varices can be counted in any individual whorl, still, as the fourth from the labrum falls very close but not exactly above it, and so on in the other whorls, three disjointed varices are thus formed, and pass *very obliquely* up the spire.

MUREX (OCINEBRA) PATRUELIS.   (Plate XXIII. fig. 6.)

Testa brevissime fusiformis, dilute fuscescens, inferne vix rimata; anfract. 7–8, *convexi, in medio angulati, costis longitudinalibus circa* 9, *mediocriter fortibus, lirisque transversis, elevatis, squamosis, inæqualibus (in anfr. penult.* 5–6, *in ultimo circiter* 13) *instructi; apertura elongata, subpyriformis, longit. totius* ½ *adæquans, intus pallide fuscescens; columella supra parum arcuata, inferne oblique tortuosa; canalis brevis, recurvus.*

Longit. 10 *millim., diam. max.* 6¼. *Apertura* 5½ *longa,* 2⅓ *lata.*

This little species is very like *M. diadema* of Aradas and Benoit, but has not the liration at the angle of the whorls produced into hollow spines upon the costæ. The liræ, also, are more numerous, and the nuclear whorls are differently sculptured. None of the few specimens at hand are quite mature, so I cannot state whether the labrum is smooth or denticulate within.

MUREX (OCINEBRA) ALBOANGULATUS.   (Plate XXI. fig. 7.)

Testa brevissime fusiformis, rufo-fusca, ad angulum anfractuum et basim anfr. ultimi alba; apex rufescens; anfr. 7, *apicales* 3 *convexi, liris tenuissimis longitudinalibus numerosis, paucisque transversis sculpti, cæteri superne declives, infra medium acute angulati, costis crassis circa* 10, *lirisque fortibus spiralibus squamulatis (in anfr. penult.* 5, *in ultimo ad* 11) *instructi; anfr. ultimus paulo infra medium contractus; columella callo albo incrassata; apertura albida, longit. totius* ½ *subæquans; labrum incrassatum, intus denticulatum.*

Longit. 8 *millim., diam. max.* 5½.

This species has the general aspect of certain *Coralliophilæ*, and might be placed with that group provisionally until the animal and operculum are known. It differs from *M. patruelis* in having smaller apical whorls, in coloration, and in sculpture, the transverse or spiral ridges being somewhat finer and more squamose.

Lachesis helenæ.   (Plate XXI. fig. 8.)

*Testa fusiformi-ovata, saturate fusca, interdum pallide flavo
zonata; anfractus 6, nuclearis corneus, convexus, lævis, cæteri
convexiusculi, sutura profunde sejuncti, costis crassis obliquis
circa* 13, *lirisque spiralibus, fortibus, supra costas granosis* (*in
anfr. superioribus* 3, *in ultimo ad* 9) *cancellati; apertura parva,
longit. totius ½ vix æquans; labrum incrassatum, intus denticulis senis munitum; columella leviter arcuata, callo tenui,
inferne ad canalem brevem obliquum albo induta.*

Longit. 7 *millim., diam. max.* 3⅓. *Apertura* 3¼ *longa,* 1½ *lata.*

This species is broader than most of the European forms. Of the
three liræ upon the upper whorls, the uppermost is rather more
slender than the other two. A fourth liration is occasionally visible
at the lower part of the whorls. The oblique ribs are more or less
regularly continuous up the spire.

Cantharus (Tritonidea) albozonatus.   (Plate XXI. fig. 9.)

*Testa breviter fusiformis, saturate purpureo-fusca, circa medium
anfractuum albo zonata, lirisque supra costas albo nodosis,
cincta; anfr.* 7–8, *superne concavi, deinde convexi, costis
crassiusculis ad* 8, *et liris spiralibus, supra costas nodulosis,
instructi; liræ in anfr. superioribus* 3–4, *duæ prope medium
albæ, aliis majores, in ultimo* 9–10; *apertura elongate pyriformis, longit. totius ½ æquans, intus lilacea, zona alba ornata;
labrum intus tenuiter liratum, liris elongatis, longe intrantibus,
haud ad marginem attingentibus; canalis angustus, obliquus,
paulo recurvus; columella supra medium arcuata, purpureo-
fusca, callo tenui, superne tuberculata, munita, inferne alba.*

Longit. 16 *millim., diam. max.* 8.

Var. *Testa brevior, saturate purpureo-fusca, nodulis flaves-
centibus supra costas, præter duas albas prope medium anfractuum, ornata.*

Longit. 11 *millim., diam. max.* 6.

This species varies considerably in form and colour. The smaller
variety has the ribs rather more numerous and is of much stumpier
growth, but the series of specimens at hand is sufficiently large to
clearly connect the two varieties. The Mediterranean *C. orbignyi*
is a larger shell, has the white zone lower down, and differs in colour
and in the aperture.

Cantharus (Tritonidea) consanguineus.   (Plate XXI.
fig. 10.)

Cominella lugubris, Jeffreys (non C. B. Adams), Melliss's St.
Helena, p. 124.

*Testa fusiformi-ovata, pallide rufescens, liris transversis,
nigrescentibus cincta; anfractus* 8–9, *apicales* 3½ *convexi,
læves, cæteri superne concavi, in medio obtuse angulati, costis
lævibus circa* 10, *lirisque supra costas nodulosis, instructi; liræ
in anfr. penultimo* 3–4, *una ad suturas, una vel duæ contiguæ*

*circa medium ; anfr. ultimus inferne contractus, subrimatus,
liris præcipuis* 6-7, *aliisque tenuibus, intercalentibus, cinctus ;
apertura parva, albida vel lilacea, cum canali longit. totius
dimidium superans; columella callo tenui, superne tuberculo
parvo munito induta ; canalis obliquus, angustus, recurvus ;
labrum intus incrassatum, liris* 6-7 *instructum.*
Longit. 14 *millim., diam. max.* 8.

This species has much of the character of two species—the one
Can. nodulosus from the West Indies, and the other *C. lugubris*
from Panama, both described by C. B. Adams. The spire of the
latter species seems to be rather longer than that of the present
species; its aperture is consequently proportionally shorter, and the
coloration is not the same. *C. nodulosus*, which is very closely
allied to the present form, besides being differently coloured, is a
somewhat more robust species and has a shorter canal, and the whorls
seem to be rather less angular.

These three forms are difficult to locate generically ; and although
I have considered them as belonging to the *Tritonidea* section of
Cantharus, they might with equal propriety be associated with
Sistrum.

CANTHARUS (TRITONIDEA) LÆVIS. (Plate XXI. fig. 11.)

*Testa fusiformi-ovata, alba, lineis transversis saturate fuscis
ornata, interque costas fusco tincta; anfr.* 10, *apicales tres
convexi, læves, flavescentes, sequentes superne concavi, in medio
angulati, infra angulum convexiusculi, costis crassis* 9, *ad
angulum acutis, instructi ; anfr. ultimus elongatus, prope
medium contractus, inferne subrimatus ; apertura alba, cum
canali longit. totius* ½ *superans; labrum extus valde incrassatum, intus denticulis ad* 6 *munitum ; columella callo albo,
tenui induta ; canalis elongatus, obliquus, recurvus.*
Longit. 23 *millim., diam. max.* 10; *apertura cum canali* 12 *longa,*
4½ *lata.*

This pretty species recalls certain forms of the genus *Siphonalia.*
It is unlike most species of *Cantharus* in having no tubercular sculpture, on which account I have called it *C. lævis.*

COLUMBELLA (ANACHIS) DECIPIENS (C. B. Adams).

Buccinum concinnum, C. B. Adams, Proc. Bost. Soc. Nat. Hist.
1845.
Columbella decipiens, C. B. Adams, Contrib. Conch. p. 55 ; Reeve,
Conch. Icon. pl. xx. fig. 111.
Col. crassilabris, Reeve, l. c. pl. xxviii. fig. 177 *a–b.*
Hab. Jamaica (*C. B. Adams*).

In the Museum are the type of *C. crassilabris* and the specimen
of *C. decipiens* figured by Reeve. They unquestionably belong to
the same species. The figure of the former is not good as regards
form, and is very greatly enlarged, although no indication of this
appears on the plate. The only specimen from St. Helena forms
part of a collection made by Mr. J. Macgillivray many years ago.

COLUMBELLA (MITRELLA) CRIBRARIA, Lamarck.

This species has a very remarkable distribution. Java Seas, Ascension Island, St. Helena, Goree, Guinea, Cuba, Barbadoes, Panama, and Mazatlan have been ascribed to it; and the British Museum, besides specimens from Goree, St. Helena, Ascension, Panama, and Mazatlan, contains series from St. Vincent's, West Indies, Guatemala, and Amboyna. Those from Guatemala were described by Reeve under the name of *C. delicata* (Conch. Icon. pl. xxvii. fig. 171), but whether from the eastern or the Pacific coast is not stated. The series from Amboyna have that locality attached to them, but I am unable to discover the source whence they were obtained, and therefore cannot vouch for the correctness of the habitat. Dr. P. P. Carpenter, in his Catalogue of Mazatlan Shells, cites among the synonymy of this species the following :—*Voluta ocellata,* Gmelin ; *Buccinum parvulum,* Dunker ; *Columbella mitriformis,* Broderip and King ; and *C. guttata,* Sowerby.

This appears to be a species which varies much in size. All the specimens from Ascension and St. Helena are small, averaging about eight or nine millimetres in length. They are almost invariably decollated, and have but four whorls remaining. The largest specimen from St. Vincent's, consisting of an equal number of whorls, is 12 millimetres long. The specimens from Goree, Amboyna, and Panama are, as a rule, broader, larger, and more solid than West-Indian or St. Helena examples.

COLUMBELLA (MITRELLA) PUSILLA, Sowerby.

Col. pusilla, Sowerby, Thes. Conch. vol. i. p. 144, pl. xl. figs. 182, 183 ; Reeve, Conch. Icon. pl. xx. figs. 109, 110, 112.

Hab. West Indies (*Sowerby*), island of St. Vincent, West Indies (*Reeve*).

This species closely resembles *C. lunata,* Say, but is a trifle more slender, marked somewhat differently, has a more thickened labrum, and a more distinct sinus above. The apex of this species is invariably brown, and the lip, especially the sinus, is usually tinted with the same colour along the edge. The single specimen from St. Helena was collected by J. Macgillivray.

COLUMBELLA (MITRELLA) SANCTÆ-HELENÆ. (Pl. XXI. fig. 12.)

Testa fusiformi-ovata, parva, albida, dilute fusco lineata vel maculata, frequenter infra suturam et circa medium anfr. ultimi niveo notata; anfr. 8–9, primi 3–4 convexi, læves, cæteri parum convexi, striis spiralibus, subdistantibus insculpti, incrementi lineis striati ; anfr. ultimus infra peripheriam rotundatam contractus, oblique tenuiterque sulcatus, apertura angusta, longit. totius ½ haud æquans ; labrum mediocriter incrassatum, intus denticulis 7–8 munitum ; columella callosa, prope medium tuberculo pliciforme instructa ; canalis obliquus, brevis, recurvus.

Longit. 7½ *millim., diam. max.* 3.

The spiral subdistant striæ will readily distinguish this species

from some others which closely approach it in outline. Most of
the specimens are rather smaller than that of which the dimensions
are given above, and have an average length of 6⅓ millimetres and a
diameter of 2¾. All of this smaller form are blotched irregularly
with pale brown, and have a more or less distinct interrupted pallid
zone at the periphery, and white spots below the suture. The
larger form is ornamented with numerous longitudinal light brown
lines, which vary in thickness, and are connected, more or less, by
short transverse ones, producing somewhat the appearance of an
indistinct network.

NASSA SANCTÆ-HELENÆ, A. Adams.

A series of about forty specimens of *Nassa* from St. Helena
makes it extremely difficult to decide to which species they should be
assigned. Some exactly resemble Adams's type (Reeve, Conch. Icon.
fig. 188), whilst others appear altogether different, the form and
sculpture being very variable. The typical form may be thus
described :—Shell elongate, with a rather acutely produced spire, of
a dirty whitish colour, with a dark brown line interrupted by the
costæ around the middle of the body-whorl, also one above near the
suture, and another round the base, both being less clearly defined
and not so regularly interrupted as the median line ; whorls 8, the
three apical smooth, glassy, very convex, the rest narrowly somewhat
excavated or concave above, then moderately convex at the sides ;
sculpture consisting of 10-12 slightly oblique strongish costæ, a
little nodose at the angle of the concavity, and of spiral sulci, which
are well defined and cover the whole of the spire, but become a
trifle obsolete on the central part of the body-whorl ; outer lip
thickened by a broad external varix, marked with a brown spot, the
termination of the central interrupted line, and furnished within with
about a dozen fine liræ ; columella covered with a callus, with a
small elongate narrow tubercle above and several irregular transverse rugosities and tubercles from thence downwards. Length 12
millim., greatest diameter 6½. The principal variations consist of
differences of form and colour, in the number of costæ, and in the
greater or less development of the spiral grooving. When the spiral
sulci are strongly marked, the costæ become somewhat nodulous as
in *N. incrassata*, Ström, with which species Jeffreys, in his account of
Mr. Melliss's shells, associated two specimens obtained at St. Helena,
and placed in the British Museum by that gentleman. Not one of
the St. Helena shells has the canal stained with black like the
majority of specimens of *incrassata*.

NASSA CINCTELLA, A. Adams.

Hab. St. Helena, 20 fathoms, sandy mud (*Adams*).

The two specimens in Mr. Cuming's collection are all I have seen of
this species. It is rather like the West-Indian *N. ambigua* of
Montagu in its short squarish form, but differs in having less tabulated whorls, and stronger or coarser spiral sculpture.

CORALLIOPHILA ERYTHROSTOMA. (Plate XXIII. fig. 7.)

Testa brevis, alba, brevissime fusiforme; anfractus 6, tabulati, in medio angulati, costis 8–9 paulo obliquis et liris spiralibus pulcherrime squamulatis (in anfr. superioribus ad 6, in ultimo circa 15) instructi; anfr. ultimus inferne angustatus, rimam angustam umbilicalem exhibens; apertura pyriformis, longe intus rufescens; labrum album, intus sulcatum; columella superne parum arcuata, infra medium obliqua; canalis mediocris, paulo recurvus. Operculum ignotum.

Longit. 22 *millim.; diam. max.* 15, *min.* 12. *Apertura* 14 *longa,* 6 *lata.*

This species is chiefly distinguished by its short broad-shouldered form, and the reddish interior of the mouth. The liration upon the costæ at the angle is rather acutely produced, giving it a pretty festooned appearance.

CORALLIOPHILA ATLANTICA. (Plate XXIII. fig. 8.)

Testa fusiformi-ovata, rimata, alba, mediocriter crassa; anfr. 6, convexi, costis obliquis circiter 11, plerumque parum elevatis, lirisque spiralibus, minute squamatis (in anfr. superioribus circa 4, in ult. ad 20 irregulariter alternatim majoribus) instructi; apertura subpyriformis, alba, longit. totius ⅓ superans; labrum intus sulcatum; columella rectiuscula; canalis brevis.

Longit. 17 *millim.; diam.* 11.   *Apertura* 11½ *longa,* 4½ *lata.*
     ,,   13   ,,   ,,   8½   ,,   7½ ,,   3½ ,,

This species is chiefly distinguished by the roundness of the whorls and the slight development of the costæ; in some specimens they are all but obsolete.

CORALLIOPHILA BRACTEATA (Brocchi).

Hab. Mediterranean.

The two little specimens from St. Helena of this variable species belong to var. 4 as described by Monterosata (*vide* ' Nuova revista Conch. Medit.' 1875, p. 40, as *Pseudomurex*). *Murex gravesii*, Broderip (Proc. Zool. Soc. 1836, p. 44), as pointed out by Tryon, is another synonym of this variety.

PURPURA HELENA, Q. & G.

? *Purpura undata*, Lamarck, Anim. s. Vert. vol. vii. p. 238.

Purpura helena, Quoy & Gaimard, Voy. Astrolabe, Zool. vol. i. (1832) p. 573, Atlas, pl. 39. figs. 7–10.

Purpura bicarinata, Blainville, Nouv. Ann. du Muséum d'Hist. Nat. vol. i. (1832) p. 215.

Purpura fasciata, Reeve, Conch. Icon. vol. iii. pl. ix. fig. 45.

Purpura undata, Kiener (partim), Icon. Coq. Viv. pl. 34. figs. 81 a–c.

Cuma carinifera, Tryon (partim), Man. Conch. vol. i. pl. 62. fig. 324.

Hab. West Indies (*Küster, Higgins & Marrat,* and *British*

Museum) ; Ascension Island (*Conry*) ; Cape Verde Islands (*Mac-Andrew*).

The specimens collected by Mr. Melliss at St. Helena and named by Jeffreys *P. rudolphi* (Ann. & Mag. Nat. Hist. 1872, April, p. 264) belong to this species. St. Helena examples are generally of a darker colour than those from the West Indies, but they agree in nearly always having a purple-brown stain on the edge of the columella bordering the canal. This seems to be a fairly constant character. *Purpura forbesii*, Dunker (Index Moll. Guinea, p. 22), is very close to, if not the same as, this species.

The shell described by Quoy and Gaimard is scarcely half-grown, and has a very different appearance from the adult worn specimen figured in the ' Conchologia Iconica ' as *P. fasciata*. The series of specimens in the British Museum clearly shows, however, that both are merely different stages of one and the same species.

MITRA (CANCILLA) TURTONI.   (Plate XXII. fig. 1.)

Testa fusiformis, dilute olivaceo-fusca, spiraliter crebre lirata et sulcata, in sulcis longitudinaliter striata ; anfractus 10, apicales tres aut quatuor lævigati, pallidi, cæteri leviter convexi ; apertura rubescens, longit. totius ½ æquans ; columella paulo obliqua, plicis 4–5 in medio instructa.

Longit. 27 *millim., diam. max.* 8 *; apertura* 13½ *longa, fere* 3 *lata.*

This species is considerably like *M. gambiana*, Dohrn, as regards form, but differs in colour and sculpture, the sulci being deeper, and the intervening liræ narrower. The fine longitudinal striæ are chiefly visible in the grooves, but they do to some extent cross the riblets.

MITRA (TURRICULA) INNOTABILIS.   (Plate XXIII. fig. 9.)

Testa parva, fusca, lira alba circa medium anfr. ultimi ornata ; anfractus 6, nucleus magnus, convexus, nitidus, anfr. sequentes paulo convexi, costis obliquis circa 12, lirisque spiralibus, supra costas nudulosis (in anfr. superioribus 3, ultimo circiter 12) instructi ; apertura angusta, longit. totius ½ haud æquans ; columella triplicata, callo tenui amicta ; labrum tenue, intus læve.

Longit. 7 *millim., diam* 2⅕.; *apertura* 3 *longa,* 1 *lata.*

The cancellation is coarse for so small a shell. The whorls have a slightly turreted appearance, being divided by a deep suture. The white liration is the third from the top of the whorls.

MITRA (PUSIA) SANCTÆ-HELENÆ.   (Plate XXII. fig. 2.)

Testa parva, brevis, ovata, alba, inter nodulos nigro fasciata ; anfractus 5, primus lævis, globosus, nigrescens, cæteri convexiusculi, sutura subprofunda sejuncti, costis confertis, granulosis, sulcis spiralibus sculptis instructi ; costæ circiter 16, vix obliquæ, fere ad basim anfr. ultimi productæ ; sulci angusti, subæquales, in anfr. superioribus 2–3, in ultimo 10–12 ; apertura parva,

*longit. totius ½ æquans; labrum leviter incrassatum, intus den-
ticulatum; columella triplicata.*

Longit. 5 millim., *diam* 2¼.

This species at first sight looks very like the shell previously
described as *Pleurotoma multigranosa*, but, of course, is perfectly
distinct. It is remarkable for its small size, the minutely beaded
ribs, the dark apex, and the style of coloration. Allied to *M. albo-
cincta*, C. B. Adams.

MITRA (THALA) PLEUROTOMOIDES. (Plate XXIII. fig. 10.)

*Testa parva, breviter fusiformis, albida, interdum luteo-tincta;
anfractus sex, duo supremi læves, superne acute carinati, plani,
quasi truncati, cæteri convexiusculi, costis longitudinalibus
circiter 16, lirisque transversis (in anfr. penult. 5–6, in ultimo
18–20) granose clathrati; apertura parva, angusta, longit.
totius ½ adæquans; labrum leviter incrassatum, denticulis circiter
sex intus munitum, postice distincte sinuatum; columella rectiuscula, leviter obliqua, in medio plicis duobus instructa, callo
tenui superne labro juncto induta.*

Longit. 5 millim., *diam.* 2.

This species is remarkable for the peculiar truncate apex, the
Pleurotomoid labral sinus, and the columellar plaits being two only
in number. Fischer (Man. Conch. p. 612) has pointed out that
Mitras of the group *Thala* have much affinity with the shells of
Clathurella and *Mangilia*. I might point out that one species,
Thala solida, was described by Reeve[1] as belonging to the latter
genus, and another, *Thala todilla*, was originally published by
Mighels[2] as a species of *Pleurotoma*. It therefore still remains
doubtful to which family, *Pleurotomidæ* or *Mitridæ*, this group
should be referred.

MARGINELLA (VOLVARIA) CINEREA, Jousseaume.

The type of this species, *M. semen* of Reeve, not of Lea, described
by Reeve (Conch. Icon. pl. xxvi. fig. 145), is now in the Museum,
having been presented by Mrs. Lombe Taylor after the death of her
husband. It is incorrectly said by Reeve to have four plaits on the
columella, for on careful examination only three are discernible,
nor is this number exceeded in any of the specimens, nearly twenty
in number, from St. Helena. Reeve's figure does not accurately
represent the form of the spire, and the sutural line is too low down.
No locality has previously been quoted for it.

MARGINELLA (VOLVARIA) CONSANGUINEA. (Plate XXIII.
fig. 11.)

*Testa minuta, ovata, alba, nitida, pellucida; anfractus 3–4; spira
brevissima, obtusissime conica; anfr. ultimus elongate ovatus, in
medio labri levissime constrictus; apertura angustissima;
labrum paulo incrassatum, inflexum, arcuatum, intus læve,*

[1] Conch. Icon. (*Mangelia*), sp. 64.
[2] Proc. Bost. Soc. Nat. Hist. 1845, vol. i. p. 24.

*superne suturam haud attingens ; columella inferne triplicata,
plica suprema minima, interdum subobsoleta.*
Longit. 2½ *millim., lat.* 1½.
M. *lavulliana* of d'Orbigny, a common West-Indian species,
appears to more closely resemble this than any other. That form
is, however, a little more solid, hardly so narrow, and has four or
more folds on the columella.

MARGINELLA (VOLVARIA) ATOMUS.   (Plate XXIII. fig. 12.)

*Testa minuta, pyriformi-ovata, alba, pellucida, lævis ; spira obtu-
sissima, vix elata ; apertura angusta ; labrum paulo inflexum et
incrassatum, superne suturæ junctum, intus haud denticulatum ;
columella quadriplicata, plica suprema minutissima.*
Longit. 1½ *millim., lat.* 1.
This species might almost be regarded as a small form of the
Australian M. *angasi*, from which it seems to differ chiefly in size.
The columella of that species is not quite the same, however, being
furnished with a few additional denticles or plicæ at the upper
part.

CASSIS TESTICULUS, var.

Hab. West Indies.
The St. Helena form of this species is that named *C. crumena* by
Bruguière. From the series of specimens examined, I am inclined
to think that it cannot be held distinct. It appears to exist on the
eastern side of the Atlantic, and has not, I think, been recorded from
the western parts. The typical form, however, of *C. testiculus* is
known from the West-African coast, and a specimen from that
region was presented to the Museum by F. P. Marrat, Esq.

TRITON TRITONIS (Linné).

Hab. W. Indies, Mediterranean, N. Australia, Pacific Islands.
A single specimen in a very worn and broken condition, and
which, when perfect, must have been about twelve inches in
length, is all that was found by Capt. Turton at St. Helena.
Mr. Melliss "obtained two living specimens which came ashore
at Lemon Valley." The species occurs also at the Canary and
Cape de Verde Islands, and it is well known from the West-Indian
region. *T. seguenzæ*, Aradas and Benoit, is, in my opinion, the
Mediterranean variety of this species.

TRITON OLEARIUM (Linné).

Hab. New Zealand, Port Jackson, Japan, Tahiti, West Indies,
Mediterranean, &c., &c.
The distribution of this species is truly remarkable, and has been
ably discussed by Lischke [1].
The specimens from St. Helena have the spiral ridges much more
prominently nodose than usual, the varices are thicker, and the
labrum not effuse, but very solid and strong as in *T. aquatilis*. In

---

[1] Japan, Meeres-Conchyl. part i. p. 48.

colour, however, the columella and the denticles within the outer lip exactly resemble *T. olearium*. *T. aquatilis* (Reeve, Conch. Icon. fig. 24) has a great affinity with *T. pilearis* (Reeve, *l. c.* fig. 23), and both have an equally wide range. Both occur at the Philippine Is., Japan, the Red Sea, and the West Indies; and the general structure of the two forms is so very similar, that I am inclined to think that eventually, when large series can be re-examined, it will be impossible to distinguish them. The shell in the d'Orbigny collection marked "*T. martinianum*, d'Orb."[1], is quite a typical *aquatilis*, and his three examples of *T. americanum*[2] from Rio Janeiro, which he formerly considered *T. pilearis*[3], certainly belong to *T. olearium*.

The largest specimen from St. Helena, which is much broken, when perfect must have measured about four and a half inches in length.

TRITON TURTONI. (Plate XXI. figs. 13, 13 *a*.)

Testa elongata, fusiformis, turrita, rufescens, varicibus albidis, rufo-zonatis, instructa; anfr. 11, *embryonales* 6 *pallide fusci, convexi, cæteri superne tabulati, angulati, inferne ad suturam valde constricti, liris spiralibus, costis longitudinalibus, nodosis, rotundatis, varicibusque paucis instructi; costæ ad angulum prominentes (in anfract. penultimo* 7), *in ultimo infra medium obsoletæ; liræ transversæ, inæquales; apertura longe intus lurida, cum canali longit. totius* ½ *æquans; labrum intus album, liris circiter* 6 *instructum, ad marginem paribus senis denticulorum partim fusco-tinctorum armatum; columella in medio arcuata, plus minus purpureo-nigra, rugis transversis, gracilibus, albis ornata; canalis intus albus, recurvus.*

Longit. 49 *millim., lat.* 20.

This is a very distinct species, and well characterized by the angled tabulated whorls which are much constricted at the lower suture. On the five normal whorls there are only four varices, two on the body-whorl and two on the penultimate. Of the spiral ridges, one marking the angle and one below it, and which are nodose upon the costæ, are most conspicuous.

RANELLA CÆLATA, Broderip.

This species is common on the coast of Panama, and it is extremely remarkable that it should occur at St. Helena. The single specimen collected by Mr. Melliss[4], and presented to the British Museum, corresponds in every particular with Panama examples; but those obtained by Capt. Turton partly belong to the same variety, and partly to that named *R. pustulosa* by Reeve, from Ascension Island, which differs from the Panama type in having fewer and larger tubercles. A specimen collected by Staff-Surgeon

---

[1] Sagra's Hist. Cuba, Mollusques, vol. ii. p. 162.
[2] Voy. dans l'Amér. Mérid., Moll. p. 711.
[3] *Ibid.* p. 449.
[4] *Vide* Jeffreys, Ann. Mag. Nat. Hist. 1872, vol. ix. p. 264.

T. Conry at Ascension, and presented by him to the British
Museum, has, however, tubercles as in *R. cælata.* The number of
the nodules seems to be very variable, and a character of no specific
importance. With this species may also be united *R. ponderosa,*
Reeve, the locality of which was unknown to its author, and some
shells labelled *R. quercina,* Mörch[1], in Cuming's collection, said
to have come from Guinea, evidently belong to the same species.
As I have been unable to consult the work of Schröter, referred to
by Mörch, who gives no description of his species, I cannot say
whether these specimens are correctly identified. They are peculiar
in having the nodules on the upper whorls as in typical specimens.

RANELLA THOMÆ, d'Orbigny.

Hab. St. Thomas (*d'Orbigny*) ; Madeira (*Watson*) ; Canary
Islands ('*Challenger*') ; Cape Verde Islands (*Brit. Mus.*); Mauritius (*Robillard*).

D'Orbigny's description of this species (Sagra's Hist. Cuba,
Moll. vol. ii. p. 164) was based upon an old dead specimen, entirely
devoid of colour, now in the British Museum. In fresh examples
the aperture is tinted with pale rose, and the varices and spiral
ridges are irregularly spotted and dotted with brown. The enlarged
figure in the above-mentioned work (pl. xxiii. fig. 23) is not at all
good. The labrum is not so bulging, the granules are not so bead-
like, the body-whorl is more constricted below, the varix on the
left, and the basal canal is directed to the right and not to the left.
The largest specimen in the Museum is from St. Vincent, Cape
Verde Islands, and measures 22 millim. in length.

This species also occurs at the Mauritius, and has been named
R. bergeri[2]. This distribution supports Tryon's opinion, that
R. thomæ should be considered to be the same as *R. rhodostoma,* and
indeed, excepting that the brown dotting is more conspicuous and
the colour of the aperture different, there is little to found specific
distinction upon. I cannot, however, agree with that author in
considering *R. cruentata* and *R. rhodostoma* forms of one and the
same species.

NATICA TURTONI.   (Plate XXI. figs. 14, 14 a.)

*Testa globosa, late umbilicata, rufescens, plus minus radiatim
strigata, zonis quatuor albis, maculis saturate fusco-rufis,
quadratis, interruptis, cincta, striis incrementi, ad suturam leviter
plicatis, sculpta, epidermide decidua, sublamellata, induta;
anfractus 4–5, celeriter accrescentes, convexi, sutura profunda
sejuncti, ultimus magnus, aperturam versus leviter expansus vel
tubiformis ; umbilicus albus, magnus, callo mediocriter tenui in
medio instructus ; apertura dilatata, semicircularis, intus albida,
coloribus externis leviter conspicuis.*
Diam. maj. 19 *millim., min.* 14, *alt.* 18.

[1] Cat. Conch. Yoldi, p. 106.
[2] Canefri, Mém. Soc. Malac. Belgique, 1880, vol. xv. p. 50, pl. 2. figs. 1, 2.

*Operculum calcarium, ex anfractibus duobus constitum, inferne
   læve, incrementi lineis striatum, extus porcis spiralibus septenis
   valde inæqualibus, sulcis interjicientibus profundis, instructum.*
   (Plate XXI. fig. 14 a.)

In *style* of coloration this species resembles *N. tæniata*, the
well-known species from the Indian Ocean and the Philippines. It
is, however, of a slightly different form, and the colour, both
externally and within the aperture, is dissimilar. The two forms are
at once distinguishable by the opercula.

The operculum of *N. tæniata* (Plate XXI. fig. 15) is externally
grooved and ridged, like that of *N. turtoni*, but the ridges are more
numerous and more equal in size. The figures on Plate XXI. show
at a glance the difference. The operculum of *N. tæniata* has not
previously been described. The specimen figured was collected at
Aden by the Rev. A. W. Baynham, who, in 1885, presented to the
British Museum a very interesting series of shells from that locality.

NATICA DILLWYNII, Payraudeau.

Hab. Mediterranean in many places; Mauritius (*Robillard*);
South Pacific Islands (*B. B. Woodward*).

After carefully comparing Maltese specimens of this species with
examples of the West-Indian *N. proxima* of C. B. Adams, I am
quite convinced that they all belong to one and the same species.
Philippi (see Küster's Conch.-Cab. Monog. *Natica*, p. 123) holds
them distinct, observing that *N. proxima* is more ovate in form, and
that the umbilical ridge is much thicker and situated below the
middle of the umbilicus. In answer to this, I would observe that
these differences do not exist in specimens in the Cumingian Collection, sent by C. B. Adams himself. None of the St. Helena
specimens are full-sized, but several are very brightly coloured.

In the British Museum is a single specimen sent direct from the
Mauritius by M. Robillard, which is absolutely identical with West-
Indian examples with which I have compared it, and specimens from
the South-Pacific Islands shown to me by Mr. Woodward seem to
belong undoubtedly to this species.

NATICA SANCTÆ-HELENÆ.   (Plate XXI. fig. 16.)

*Testa parva, umbilicata, globularis, nitida, albida, zona interrupta
   rufo-fusca infra suturam cincta, lineis pallidioribus, ziczac-
   formibus, prope umbilicum saturatioribus, zonam indistinctam
   formantibus, ornata; anfractus 5, rapide accrescentes; spira
   parva, parum prominens; umbilicus parvus, callo columellari
   albido semiobtectus; apertura semicircularis.*

Alt. 9 *millim., diam. max.* 9.

This species probably attains a larger size than the above dimensions indicate. It resembles *N. alderi* of Forbes in form, excepting
that the tip of the spire is scarcely so pointed, but the style of
markings may be sufficiently different to distinguish it. Besides the
rich brown, more or less interrupted zone beneath the suture, and
the less distinct one around the umbilicus, the angles of the zigzag

lines also form two or three spiral bands. The thickened border of the umbilicus is not stained with brown so distinctly as in *N. alderi*. The operculum is at present unknown.

NATICA (POLINICES) PORCELLANA, d'Orbigny.

Hab. Teneriffe, Madeira, Cape Verde Islands.

This species and *N. uberina* of the same author from the West Indies are very closely related, but the majority of specimens of the latter have a differently formed callus. The figure in Sagra's 'Hist. Cuba' (pl. xvii. fig. 19) represents an umbilical callus very like that of *N. porcellana*, but in most West-Indian specimens it has not got such a central prominence at the termination of the umbilical ridge, and consequently a less marked sinus above it.

All the specimens from St. Helena are much smaller than the type figured by d'Orbigny (Webb & Berthelot's Hist. Nat. Canaries, Mollusques, pl. vi. figs. 27, 28).

The umbilicus also in these specimens is unusually large, the groove within it deep, and the curved ridge is rather sharp. In the specimen of *N. porcellana* figured by Reeve (Conch. Icon. figs. 102 *a*, *b*) the umbilicus is much narrower and the callosity more developed. In the Museum Collection there are two specimens from Goree, named *N. loveni*, Dunker, which undoubtedly belong to this species, but at present I have not met with any description of that species. The operculum is thin, horny, and reddish. In his list of St. Helena shells Jeffreys quotes *N. nitida*, Donovan. We did not receive this shell from Mr. Melliss; but it is possible it may have been the present species, which is not unlike Donovan's figure.

IANTHINA COMMUNIS, Lamarck.

Hab. East and West Atlantic.

This species appears in Jeffreys's list of Mr. Melliss's St. Helena shells under the name of *I. fragilis*. The form and colour varies considerably in the seven specimens from the shores of St. Helena. Some are as depressed as *I. cœrulcata*, Reeve (Conch. Icon. figs. 7*a*, 7*b*), and similarly coloured, whilst others are much more elevated, nearly as high in the spire as *I. africana*, Reeve, fig. 8 *a*, *b*, and white above as in that species, which is also considered but a variety of the present species by Sowerby (Thesaurus, v. p. 56). *I. bicolor*, Lesson [1], also described and figured from St. Helena specimens, belongs to this species.

IANTHINA GLOBOSA, Swainson.

Hab. St. Helena (*Lesson*).

This species is described and figured by Lesson, from examples taken at St. Helena, under the name of *I. prolongata*, Blainville (*vide* Voy. Coquille, Zool. vol. ii. p. 366).

---

[1] Zool. Voy. Coquille, vol. ii. p. 365.

IANTHINA EXIGUA, Lamarck.

Hab. South Atlantic; " New Zealand, New South Wales, and S. Australia " (*Hutton*).

I have compared New-Zealand specimens in the Museum with the one from St. Helena, and can discover no distinction.

IANTHINA UMBILICATA, d'Orbigny.

Ianthina umbilicata, d'Orb. Sagra's Hist. Cuba, Mollusq. vol. ii. p. 85, Atlas, pl. xx. figs. 22, 23 (bad !) ; id. Voy. Amér. Mérid. vol. v. p. 414 ; Reeve, Con. Icon. figs. 22*a*, *b* ; Sowerby, Thesaurus, pl. 444. fig. 22.

> *Testa parva, violacea, infra suturam albo anguste zonata, anguste perforata*; *anfractus 5, primi duo (nucleus) obliqui, parvi, papilliformes, pellucidi, cæteri convexi, nitidi, ultimus in medio obtuse angulatus et sulcatus, incrementi lineis, in medio angulatis, sculptus; apertura mediocris, inferne anguste effusa; columella rectiuscula, paulo reflexa; labrum profunde et acute incisum.*

Alt. 9½ *millim., diam.* 8.

The British Museum received many specimens of this species from Mr. Nuttall in the year 1855, under the name of *I. bifida*[1]. They were obtained at the Sandwich Islands. The shell figured by Reeve under that name is altogether different, and seems to me but a form of *I. exigua,* as suggested by Sowerby. Besides the lines of growth, which are perhaps a trifle coarser on the under surface than upon the spire, there are indications of feeble spiral striæ, chiefly upon the base.

The figure given by d'Orbigny is not good, and does not accord with his description. The labrum is described as acutely sinuated, and the surface as smooth, or scarcely marked with faint lines of growth, yet the figure depicts no sinuation, but represents rather well-marked incremental striæ. In d'Orbigny's South-American shells are preserved three or four specimens of this species, marked *I. umbilicata* in his own handwriting. These certainly agree with the single specimen from St. Helena and the large series from the Sandwich Islands. The figure in Reeve's ' Conchologia ' represents the form correctly, but does not show the deep labral notch. D'Orbigny describes the colour as uniform deep blue, but his specimens have the pale infrasutural line as described above.

All the specimens of this species which I have examined are of small size, none exceeding the dimensions above given.

IANTHINA PALLIDA, Harvey.

Hab. Ireland (*Thompson*); Straits of Magellan (*Jeffreys*).

The single St. Helena specimen, half an inch in length, agrees very closely with Forbes and Hanley's figure (Brit. Moll. pl. 69. figs. 10, 11).

---

[1] Blanford, ' Geology and Zoology of Abyssinia,' p. 463, gives off the S.E. coast of Arabia as a locality for this species.

SCALARIA CONFUSA.

Scalaria turricula, Sowerby, partim, Thes. Conch. vol. i. p. 92.

Hab. Catanuan, Isle of Luzon, Philippines (*Cuming*) ; Sandwich Islands (*Mus. Cuming*) ; N.W. Australia (*Capt. Beckett in Brit. Mus.*).

Sowerby seems to me to have included two species under the name *S. turricula*—the one a distinctly striated shell with unequal varices ; the other, which I now name *S. confusa,* being smooth and with more regular riblets. The true *turricula* is represented by figure 88 [1] in the 'Thesaurus,' where the thick varix on the penultimate whorl shows the spine or tooth-like projection at the upper end, a feature not occurring in *Sc. confusa.* It is only the thick riblets (former peristomes) which have the spine. 'Thesaurus,' fig. 61, fairly represents the form of the present species, but the colour is too red, the varices not fine enough, and the interstices should be smooth and not spirally striated. Fig. 59 in the 'Conch. Icon.' also gives a coarse idea of this species. The St. Helena specimens have the lower half of the whorls light brown, and the upper half dirty white, with oblique faint brown blotches, and all the riblets are white throughout. In comparison with the three specimens from N.W. Australia, those from St. Helena are a trifle more suddenly tapering ; but as both exhibit the same glossy surface similar colour, and varices, I feel convinced that they should be considered as belonging to one and the same species.

SCALARIA FRAGILIS, Hanley.

Scalaria fragilis, Hanley, Conchologist's Book of Species, p. 63 (1842) ; Sowerby, Thesaurus, vol. i. p. 88, pl. xxxiii. figs. 64–66 (1844) ; id. Conch. Icon. pl. v. fig. 29.

Scalaria albida, d'Orbigny, Sagra's Hist. Cuba, Moll. vol. ii. p. 17, pl. x. figs. 24, 25.

Hab. St. Vincent's and Cuba.

Of the five St. Helena specimens, three are rather less slender than the majority of West-Indian examples, but the two others have quite the same form. Species of *Scalaria* appear to vary in respect of proportional dimensions.

The figure in Hanley's work is not good, but I nevertheless believe that it represents the same species as that described by Sowerby. The latter is, however, certainly identical with *S. albida* of d'Orbigny, proved by a comparison of the types.

SCALARIA MELLISSI.   (Plate XXIII. fig. 13.)

Testa Sc. trevelyanæ *similis, sed paulo robustior, lamellisque longitudinalibus simplicibus, superne haud subspinosis.*
Longit. 14 *millim., diam.* 4½.

The shells here described were collected by Mr. Melliss, and appear in his list under the name of *S. modesta* of C. B. Adams.

---

[1] I retain this as the type because in both of his diagnoses the author refers to the minute spiral striation.

That species has, however, rather stronger ribs and distinct spiral striæ, which at once separate it from the present species.

S. mellissi is of a livid colour, and glossy between the white ribs, which are thirteen or fourteen in number, and are very like those of *S. trevelyanæ*, but have not the short projection near the upper end. It may be described as a stumpier species than that shell, the spire being less slender.

SCALARIA SANCTÆ-HELENÆ. (Plate XXIII. fig. 14.)

Testa parva, albida, turrita, gracilis, imperforata ; anfractus 8–9, primi 3–4 lævigati, nitentes, convexi, pellucidi, cæteri convexi, contigui, lamellis numerosis, (in anfr. ult. 26–28) tenuissimis, paulo obliquis, instructi ; apertura subcircularis, inferne obscure effusa.

Longit. 4½ *millim., diam.* 1½.

The number of whorls, and their steady enlargement, incline me to believe that this species does not attain a much larger size. It seems to approach *S. pulchella*, Bivona, but the riblets are finer and the whorls not quite so high.

SCALARIA COMMODA. (Plate XXIII. fig. 15.)

Testa parva, angusta, elongata, albida, imperforata ; anfractus 9, sutura undulata sejuncti, primi tres convexi, nitidi, rufescentes, cæteri convexi, costis crassis circa 11, *leviter obliquis, lirisque tenuibus, pluribus, cancellati, incrementi lineis minutissime decussati ; anfr. ultimus lira crassa inferne cinctus ; apertura ovato-circularis, superne quam basi angustior ; labrum valde incrassatum.*

Longit. 5 *millim., diam.* 1½.

This minute species is well characterized by its reddish apex, the strong ribs extended upward, so as to form a wavy sutural line, and the spiral liræ, producing a cancellated appearance.

SCALARIA ATOMUS. (Plate XXIII. fig. 16.)

Testa minima, brevis, anguste umbilicata, alba ; anfractus 4½, *perconvexi, sutura profunda sejuncti, primus lævis, cæteri costis tenuibus circiter* 18 *instructi ; apertura oblique ovata, basi paulo subeffusa ; peristoma in exemplis adultis continuum, margine columellari subreflexo.*

Longit. 1½ *millim., diam.* 1.

The shells here described, although so small, *appear* to be full-grown ; such may not, however, be the case.

SCALARIA MULTISTRIATA, Say ?

S. multistriata, Say, Amer. Conch. pl. 27 ; Sowerby, Thes. Conch. vol. i. p. 108, woodcut ; Gould, Invert. Mass. 1870, p. 313, cut.

Hab. U. States, W. Indies, Mediterranean.

A single specimen from St. Helena and one from the Canary Islands, in the Museum, apparently belong to this species. They are a trifle narrower in the body-whorl than the above-cited figures.

OBELISCUS DOLABRATUS (Linné).

Hab. West Indies; Cuba, Guadeloupe, and St. Lucia (*d'Orbigny*); Island of Annabon, West Africa (*Dunker*) ; Red Sea ; Indian and Pacific Oceans.

Several specimens were dredged in shallow water, 5–20 fathoms, off the north of the island, and this I believe is the only record of the appearance of this species on the eastern side of the Atlantic with the exception of Annabon Island mentioned above.

OBELISCUS SANCTÆ-HELENÆ.   (Plate XXIII. fig. 17.)

Testa elongata, subpellucido-alba, linea flavescente interdum cincta, nitida, perforata ; anfractus normales 7, convexiusculi, sutura mediocriter profunda separati ; nucleus convexus, involutus ; apertura inverse subauriformis ; columella recta, supra um- bilicum reflexa, superne plica valida instructa.

Longit. 6½ *millim., diam.* 2⅓.

This species is characterized by being perforated, by its convexish smooth whorls, and the distinct twist or plait on the upper part of the columella.   In most of the specimens at hand the slender coloured line which revolves round the middle of the body-whorl and up the spire, just above the suture, is very faint, but in a few fresher specimens it is much more distinct.   Some examples which have the lip broken away, thus permitting a further view within the aperture, exhibit two very fine spiral plaits or liræ on the columella, below the uppermost stouter one.   It becomes therefore a link, as it were, between the typical species of *Obeliscus* with three distinct folds on the columella, and *Syrnola* with only one, agreeing with the latter genus in general form and style of ornamentation.

OBELISCUS (SYRNOLA) PUMILIO.   (Plate XXII. fig. 3.)

Testa elongata, gracilis, nitida, alba, lineis paucis spiralibus pellucidis ornata, lineaque unica rufescenti cincta ; anfractus 8–9, leviter convexi, lente accrescentes, sutura simplici paulo oblique sejuncti ; nucleus globosus, pellucidus, obliquus, sinistrorsus ; apertura inverse subauriformis, basi vix effusa ; columella paulo reflexa, superne plicata, inferne arcuata.

Longit. 6⅓ *millim., diam.* 1⅓.

This species at first sight looks like a miniature of *S. cinctella,* A. Adams, from the Korea Straits.   It is, however, proportionally more slender, the aperture is longer, and is ornamented with a few spiral pellucid zones.

TURBONILLA HAROLDI.   (Plate XXIII. fig. 18.)

Testa elongato-oblonga, alba, superne leviter coarctata ; anfractus 6, planiusculi, turriti, sutura profunda sejuncti, ad marginem superiorem incrassati, costis longitudinalibus suberectis, fere æqualibus (in anfr. ult. circiter 16–18) instructi, in interstitiis minute spiraliter striati ; apertura inverse subauriformis, superne acuminata ; peristoma continuum, margine columellari

paulo reflexo, rimam umbilicalem angustam semiobtegente ; plica columellæ haud perspicua.
Longit. 2⅓ *millim., diam. fere* 1.

The fold or twist of the columella in this minute species is high up and not conspicuously developed.

TURBONILLA ASSIMILANS. (Plate XXIII. fig. 19.)

Testa elongata, gracilis, alba, nitida, subpellucida ; anfractus 9–10, convexi, lente accrescentes, costis tenuibus, gracilibus, (in anfr. penult. circiter 20) leviter obliquis, instructi, lirisque spiralibus paucis circa partem inferiorem inter costas ornati ; apex magnus, globosus ; anfr. ultimus costis basim versus obsoletis ; apertura parva, subovata ; columella leviter torta.
Longit. 4⅓ *millim., lat.* 1.

Turbonilla acicularis, A. Adams, from the Philippine Islands, and *T. pusilla,* C. B. Adams, from Jamaica, have very much the same form as the present species. The latter, however, is rather more slender, and has fewer riblets than *T. assimilans,* whilst the former has flatter whorls and coarser costæ.

TURBONILLA TRUNCATELLOIDES. (Plate XXIII. fig. 20.)

Testa elongata, solidiuscula, alba, linea flavescente circa medium anfractuum ornata ; anfract. 7, primus (apex) pellucidus, globosus, cæteri levissime convexi, sutura profunda sejuncti, costis longitudinalibus 15–16 *crassis, interstitiis latioribus, instructi ; anfr. ultimus linea secunda flavescenti infra medium cinctus ; apertura subpyriformis ; columella superne plicata ; peristoma continuum, margine columellari leviter reflexo.*
Longit. 4 *millim., diam.* 1⅓.

This species agrees in its general appearance with the section *Mormula,* but has a rather more distinct fold than *M. rissoina,* the type of this so-called genus.

TURBONILLA BRACHIA. (Plate XXIII. fig. 21.)

Testa minima, brevis, turrita, pellucida, albida, nitida ; anfractus 4½, apicales læves, convexi, tres sequentes convexiusculi, sutura profunda paulo obliqua sejuncti, costis bene arcuatis circiter 20 (in anfr. ultimo inferne attenuatis) instructi, paulo infra suturam, sulco inconspicuo, costas secanti, sculpti ; apex maximus, obtusus ; apertura ovalis, superne acuminata, longit. totius ⅓ adæquans ; columella leviter reflexa, spiraliter torta, labro callo tenui juncta.
Longit. 1½ *millim., diam.* ½.

The short stumpy form, the very large obtuse apex, the much curved ribs, and the deep suture are the principal distinguishing features of this little species.

TURBONILLA (DUNKERIA) ERITIMA. (Plate XXIII. fig. 22.)

Testa subulata, pellucida, vitrea, nitida ; anfractus normales 6, *convexi, liris longitudinalibus numerosis, arcuatis (in anfr.*

ultimo circiter 22, *inferne obsoletis*) *sulcisque duobus trans-*
versis, circa partem inferiorem, instructi; apex parvus,
globosus, involutus; apertura irregulariter ovata, basi sub-
effusa; columella vix torta, leviter reflexa.
Longit. 3 *millim., diam. fere* 1 ; *apertura* 1 *longa,* ½ *lata.*

Besides the two spiral sulci which encircle the lower part of the
whorls between the riblets, some microscopic spiral striæ are
observable at the upper part, and also upon the base of the body-
whorl. The little glassy nucleus is uncoiled and at a right angle to
the axis of the shell.

CINGULINA CIRCINATA, A. Adams.

Cingulina circinata, A. Adams, Ann. & Mag. Nat. Hist. 1860,
vol. vi. p. 414 ; Angas, Proc. Zool. Soc. 1867, p. 201.

Hab. North China, Japan, and Port Jackson.

Several small specimens of this species were obtained at St.
Helena. After a very careful examination under a microscope, I
cannot detect any difference whereby they can be distinguished from
this eastern form. The sculpture consists of three subequal spiral
ridges on each whorl, and a very fine thread borders the suture.
The nucleus is convex and sinistral, as in *Mathilda*, which I regard
as a subgenus of *Cingulina.* The finest specimen from Japan which
has been examined is 12 millim. in length, and consists of
thirteen normal whorls, whilst the largest St. Helena example is
only 5 millim. long and has eight volutions ; but had this shell been
permitted to go on growing, it would, by the addition of 5 more
whorls, have attained a length fully as great as the Japanese example.

CINGULINA (MATHILDA) QUADRICARINATA (Brocchi).

Hab. Mediterranean, Bay of Biscay, Madeira.

The distribution and references of this beautiful species are given
by Jeffreys in his report on the Mollusca of the 'Porcupine'
Expedition (Proc. Zool. Soc. 1884, p. 364). He observes that the
sculpture " varies considerably, and this has, of course, given rise to
several synonyms, including *Eglisia macandreæ* of A. Adams."
This latter species was described by H. (not *A.*) Adams [1] and has
six spiral liræ and more numerous and more delicate longitudinal
raised lines of growth. Until further specimens are obtained which
may connect the two forms I prefer to keep them separate.

The three specimens from St. Helena are small, the largest
measuring 13¼ millim. in length. They appear to be a trifle more
slender than the 'Porcupine' specimens and that figured by Kobelt
(Jahrbüch. deutsch. Mal. Gesell. 1874, pl. xi. figs. 2, 2 *a*). The
sculpture, however, is precisely similar.

The question has been raised by Mr. Watson ('Challenger' Gasteropoda, p. 499), whether the genus *Mathilda* is the same as *Cingu-*
lina of Adams ; but I cannot adopt the conclusion at which he arrives
namely, " either to suppress *Cingulina* altogether, or to retain it

[1] Proc. Zool. Soc. 1865, p. 753.

merely as a subgenus of *Mathilda*." It certainly either is or is not
the same; and presuming them to be identical, *Cingulina* must be
retained, having been published five years previous to *Mathilda*;
but should it be considered that they differ sufficiently in sculpture
to be placed in different sections, *Mathilda* and not *Cingulina* should
take subgeneric rank. I have this advantage over Mr. Watson in
knowing that the character of the apical whorls is the same in both,
as one of the specimens of *Cingulina circinata* in the Museum still
retains its nucleus.

The sculpture of this species, the type of the genus, is certainly
very unlike that of most of the known species of *Mathilda*, consisting
of strong spiral ridges, with only feeble lines of growth in the
interstices. *C. spina* of Crosse and Fischer is very closely related,
but quite distinct. Owing to the more cancellated surfaces of
Mathilda, it may be convenient at present to retain it as a section
or subgenus.

ODOSTOMIA GLAPHYRA.   (Plate XXIII. fig. 23.)

*Testa ovato-cylindracea, albo-pellucida; anfractus 5–6, apicalis
convexus, involutus, cæteri parum convexi, lævigati, sutura
mediocriter profunda, vix obliqua, sejuncti, ultimus penult.
latitudine subæquans; apertura parva, inverse auriformis,
longit. totius ⅓ subæquans; columella plus minus leviter con-
torta, in exemplis adultis callo tenui labro juncta.*

Longit. 2½ *millim., diam.* 1.

Although under an ordinary lens this species appears to be smooth,
it is in fact finely spirally striated. It is sufficiently pellucid to
allow of the columella being indistinctly visible up the spire, the
apex of which is large and obtuse.

EULIMA FUSCESCENS.   (Plate XXIII. fig. 24.)

*Testa parva, acuminata, recta, pallide fuscescens, polita; anfractus
octo, levissime convexi sutura simplice vix obliqua sejuncti, ultimus
ad medium magis convexus, mediocriter elongatus; apertura ovata,
superne acuminata; perist. tenue, inferne leviter effusum, margine columellari paulo reflexo, superne callo tenui labro juncto.*

Longit. 2½ *millim., lat. fere* 1; *apertura* ¾ *longa,* ⅓ *lata.*

This little species is peculiar on account of its colour, a rare feature
in this genus, and its short erect form.

EULIMA ATLANTICA.   (Plate XXIII. fig. 25.)

*Testa nivea, elongata, aut recta aut superne plus minus dextrorsum
vel sinistrorsum curvata; anfractus* 11–12, *fere plani, sutura
levi sejuncti; ultimus in medio curvatus, subbrevis; apertura
parva, ovata, superne acuminata; columella paulo incrassata,
reflexa, labro callo tenui juncta; labrum in medio prominens,
prope suturam haud profunde sinuatum.*

Longit. 7⅓ *millim., diam.* 2; *apertura* 2 *longa,* 1 *lata.*

This species has a less slender spire than *E. intermedia,* Cantraine,
is of a shorter and stumpier growth, and the reflection of the colu-

mella is different.   It is very like *E. aciculata*, Pease, of which
E. retrorsa, Sowerby, is a synonym.   It differs in the following
respects:—the lip is more sinuated above and more prominently
curved below, the spire is rather less acutely produced, and the
semipellucid zone beneath the suture is not so broad in proportion
to the rest of the whorl beneath.

EULIMA SUBCONICA.

Eulima conica, Sowerby (non C. B. Adams), Couch. Icon. fig. 44.

Both the figure and the description of this species are misleading,
for Mr. Sowerby was careless, especially when engaged with small
forms.   He describes the last whorl as " angulated," and a decided
angle is depicted in his figure.   The type has a much less pronounced
angulation ; the specimens from St. Helena are more like the figure,
but still not quite so bulging at the periphery.   The apical portion
of the spire is sometimes straight, occasionally curves to the left, or,
as in the type, turns to the right, not as drawn by Sowerby, who
has reversed the direction.

The aperture is neither "*rather square*" nor "*acuminated beneath*."
It should have been described as *obliquely oval* and a trifle more
acuminate *above* than below.   The columella is not "*rather tortuous*,"
but slightly curved and reflexed over the umbilical region.   Mr.
Sowerby apparently drew a bad figure and then based his description
upon it.

There are thirteen whorls in the type, which is four and a half
millimetres long.   They are separated by a distinct suture, and the
semipellucid margin, beneath it, occupies a little less than one-third
of the whorl.   The few uppermost are a trifle convex, the rest almost,
but not quite, flat.

The name *conica* was already in use for a Jamaican species of this
genus, described by C. B. Adams in his 'Contributions to Conchology,'
p. 110.   His diagnosis applies very closely to the St. Helena specimens ;
but, as I have not a specimen of this species for comparison, I, for the
present, prefer to consider them a distinct, but closely allied form, on
which account I have proposed the name *subconica*.

EULIMA GERMANA.   (Plate XXIII. fig. 26.)

*Testa minima, nitida, pellucida, plus minus leviter arcuata ; an-
fractus 9, planiusculi, sutura distincta vix obliqua discreti ;
apertura ovata, superne acuminata, longit. totius ⅓ subæquans ;
labrum prominens, arcuatum ; columella obliqua, curvata, antice
incrassata.*

Longit. 2½, *diam.* 1 *millim.*

Of this very little species, two specimens were obtained by Capt.
Turton, one somewhat more curved than the other.   This same
specimen also exhibits a continuous series of varices upon the right
side.   The pellucid zone beneath the suture in the penultimate whorl
is about half as broad as the space between it and the top of the
body-whorl.

EULIMA (SUBULARIA) FUSCOPUNCTATA.   (Plate XXI. fig. 18.)

*Testa minuta, subulata, pellucida, punctis fuscis irregulariter
notata, nitida ; spira acuminata, apice mediocriter acuto, con-
voluto ; anfractus 9, tres apicales convexi, cæteri subplani, elon-
gati, sutura obliqua sejuncti ; apertura elongata, ovata, superne
anguste acuminata, longit. totius $\frac{1}{4}$ paulo superans ; columella
obliqua, leviter incrassata et reflexa.*
Longit. 2$\frac{3}{4}$ millim., diam. $\frac{3}{4}$; apertura $\frac{3}{4}$ longa, $\frac{1}{3}$ lata.

This minute shining little species is remarkable for the minute
brownish scattered dots, which do not appear to be arranged in
regular series.

AMAURELLA CANALICULATA.   (Plate XXIII. fig. 27.)

*Testa parva, tenuis, hyalina, umbilicata, ovato-turrita ; anfr. 7,
convexi, ad suturam profunde canaliculati, læves ; apertura ovata,
paulo obliqua, longit. totius $\frac{1}{3}$ æquans ; peristoma tenue, margine columellari leviter dilatato, inferneque subeffuso.*
Longit. 3 millim., diam. 1$\frac{2}{3}$.

This remarkable shell has the first three or four whorls narrow in
proportion to the others, so that the spire has a suddenly contracted
appearance towards the top. The umbilicated base, smooth surface,
and channelled suture well distinguish this species. In describing
the genus *Amaurella*, Adams states incorrectly that it is "*imperforata*,"
for the typical species *A. japonica* is distinctly perforate, although
more narrowly than that now described.

CIONISCUS UNICUS (Montagu).

Hab. British Islands, west coasts of France, and some parts of
the Mediterranean.

The three specimens of this beautiful shell from St. Helena have
the whorls the least trifle shorter than British specimens with which
they have been compared, but agree in all other respects.

ACLIS ANGULATA.   (Plate XXIII. fig. 28.)

*Testa minuta, elongata, turrita, alba ; anfr. 6, primi duo magni,
convexi, læves, cæteri superne oblique declives, in medio acute
carinato-angulati, infra angulum contracti, lineis incrementi
conspicuis, elevatis, confertissimis, regularibus, sculpti ; anfr.
ultimus ad peripheriam obtusissime rotunde angulatus ; apertura
obliqua, irregulariter ovata ; peristoma continuum, haud incrassatum, supra angulum, prope suturam, leviter sinuatum.*
Longit. 2 millim., diam. $\frac{3}{4}$.

This little species is remarkable for its angular whorls, the regular
close-set raised lines of growth, and large apex.

ACLIS SIMILLIMA.   (Plate XXIII. fig. 29.)

*Testa minuta, gracilis, alba, nitida, pellucida; anfractus normales 7,
convexiusculi, sutura obliqua profunde sejuncti ; nucleus magnus,
convolutus, elevatus ; apertura lata, inverse subauriformis ;*

peristoma fere continuum, margine columellari paulo prominente, superne torto.

Longit. 2½ *millim., diam.* ½.

This minute species is very like *A. nitidissima* of Montagu, but has decidedly less convex whorls, the aperture is broader, and the columellar twist different. The heterostrophe apical coil is also very similar in both forms.

ACLIS DIDYMA.   (Plate XXIII. fig. 30.)

Testa minuta, turrita, albida, imperforata ; anfractus 6, supremus lævis, convexus, obtusus, cæteri superne declives, subexcavati, dein obtuse angulati, inferne planiusculi, longitudinaliter striati, ad angulum subplicati ; apertura parva, ovata, longit. totius ¼ adæquans ; columella levissime reflexa, superne subtorta.

Longit. 2¼ *millim., diam.* ⅔.

Owing to the large size of the nuclear whorl, this species has very gently converging outlines. The columella does not unite above with the outer lip, but appears to be slightly spirally intorted.

SOLARIUM PLACENTALE, Hinds, var.

Hab. Bay of Magdalena, California. Off Barbados in deep water (Dall for *S. peracutum*).

Three specimens in excellent condition, one alive with the operculum, were dredged by Capt. Turton. This is another instance of remarkable distribution in this genus. After a careful study and comparison of these examples with the types of *S. placentale*, and Mr. Dall's description and figures of *S. peracutum* [1], although slight differences are noticeable, I can but regard all of them as forms of one and the same species. The St. Helena specimens are a little paler in colour than the type; the periphery is perhaps very slightly more acute, as is the case with *S. peracutum* ; the crenulations bordering the umbilicus finer, and the spiral sculpture, more especially on the upper surfaces, is rather more inclined to be granular.

The operculum consists of six whorls, which rapidly increase from a central nucleus, and, on the external surface, have the outer margin elevated, forming a sutural keel and thus giving them a concave aspect. The inner surface is glossy and furnished with a strong whitish central elevated process, from which a conspicuous curved ridge arises, forming rather more than a semicircle.

The figure of *S. placentale* in the 'Conchologia Iconica' is a mere caricature, being both out of drawing and exaggerated in colour and sculpture. The figures in the 'Voyage of the Sulphur' (pl. xiv. figs. 5, 6) are good and of the natural size.

The acuteness of the peripherial keel is variable, for, in a second specimen of the typical form, received by the British Museum from Sir E. Belcher, it is sharper and flatter above.

SOLARIUM ORDINARIUM.   (Plate XXI. figs. 17–17 *b*.)

Testa orbiculo-conoidea, depressa, mediocriter umbilicata, albida

[1] Bull. Mus. Comp. Zool. Harvard, vol. xviii. p. 275, pl. xxxiii. figs. 2, 5.

*vel lilaceo tincta, rufo punctata; anfractus 5, vix convexiusculi,
liris quinque, oblique granosis cincti, ultimus ad peripheriam
acute angulatus, plerumque lilaceus, concentrice sulcatus et cingu-
latus, cingulo circa umbilicum maximo, fortiter crenato, cæteris
quoque plus minus crenulatis vel subquadrate granulatis; apertura trapeziformis, ad columellam bicanaliculata.*

Diam. max. 13 *millim., alt.* 6½.

The liræ on the upper surface, which do not vary much in size,
are cut across by deep oblique lines of growth, so that the granules
have an oblique appearance. Those on the ridges of the under
surface are squarer, as the incremental striæ are radiating.

The granules on the stout lira bordering the umbilicus are much
the coarsest, those on the other ridges becoming finer the more
remote they are from the centre.

This species has less convex whorls than *S. granulatum*, Lamarck,
from the West Indies, not such a deep suture, and considerably
finer granulation. It seems to be larger than the Mediterranean
S. moniliferum, Bronn [1], to have a different kind of granules, and the
aperture is distinctly channelled both at the lower and upper end of
the columella.

SOLARIUM HYBRIDUM, Linné.

Hab. China Sea, Philippine and Malacca Islands, Java, Ceylon,
Moreton Bay, Queensland, and New South Wales.

In separating the Mediterranean from the Australian form of
S. luteum under the name of *S. conulus*, Weinkauff [2] appears to
have been mainly influenced by difference of locality. The same
might be done in the present instance, for this is, I believe, the first
record of *S. hybridum* from the Atlantic Ocean. Only two small
specimens are in the collection; but these undoubtedly belong to this
species, possessing all the characters of colouring and sculpture met
with in eastern examples.

SOLARIUM ARCHITÆ, Costa.

Hab. Throughout the Mediterranean and in the Atlantic, off the
coast of France and Portugal.

This well-known Mediterranean species has not been previously
recorded from so southern a locality as St. Helena. I have carefully
examined the type of *S. soverbii*, Hanley, and agree, with Monterosato [3] and Jeffreys [4], in considering it the same as this species.

CYPRÆA LURIDA, Linné.

This species, which occurs in the Mediterranean, at the Azores,
the Canary and Cape Verde Islands, and on the African coast, as far
as Guinea, has not been met with further south than St. Helena.
It has also been recorded from Ascension Island by Lister, and was
obtained there by Dr. Conry. Dunker has quoted it from Annabon
Island.

---

[1] Monterosato, Notizie Solarii Mediterr. p. 5.
[2] Conch. Mittelmeer. vol. ii. p. 261.
[3] Notizie Solarii Mediter. p. 11.   [4] Proc. Zool. Soc. 1885, p. 39.

CYPRÆA SPURCA, Linné.

The distribution of this species is similar to that of the preceding, excepting that it also occurs at the West Indies (d'Orbigny and others). The single shell received from Mr. Melliss, and named *C. turdus* by Jeffreys, is merely a small specimen of *C. spurca*.

LITTORINA MILIARIS, Quoy and Gaimard (var.).

Hab. Ascension Island (Q. & G.); also R. Trimen and Dr. Conry in British Museum.

The specimens from St. Helena do not agree exactly with those from Ascension. In them the last whorl is rather less ventricose; the spire longer, and consequently more acutely conical; the aperture is a trifle more effuse at the base, and the tuberculation much less pronounced; indeed, in some instances, the surface is all but smooth. Jeffreys and Melliss have classed the St. Helena forms under the name of *L. striata*, King, but, in my opinion, they are certainly more closely related to *L. miliaris*. In connexion with this species I would observe that *L. granularis*, Gray, and *L. nodosa*, Reeve (not of Gray), are synonymous. Some remarks by Watson (Voy. ' Challenger,' Rep. Gasteropoda, p. 576) and Lischke (Japan. Meeres-Conch. ii. p. 70) have been given concerning the synonymy of *L. granularis*. After a very careful comparison of Gray's much worn type with specimens of *L. miliaris* from Ascension, I feel convinced of their identity; but I rather incline with Lischke to hold Dunker's *L. exigua*, from Japan, as distinct from *L. granularis*, Gray, with which it is united by Watson.

It is not surprising that Lischke should consider Reeve's *L. granularis* a distinct species from Gray's, seeing that the latter author's type is in such worn condition, so that neither the colour nor sculpture could be accurately described; and, moreover, it was from an unknown locality.

The very young specimens from St. Helena have quite a different aspect from the adult Ascension examples, having an angular bodywhorl and an effuse columella at the base; still, in a large series of different ages, the transitions or links are observable.

LITTORINA HELENÆ, Melliss. (Plate XXI. fig. 19.)

Littorina helenæ, Melliss's St. Helena, p. 125.

Testa parva, trochiformis, fusco-nigra, inferne regionem versus umbilici pallidior; spira elevata, conica, acuta, lateribus rectilinearibus; anfr. 8, plani, seriebus granulorum tribus ornati, striisque intercalatis paucis sculpti; anfr. ultimus subacute angulatus, ad angulum serie tuberculorum duplici instructus, inferne liris concentricis tenuibus cinctus; apertura parva, rotunde quadrata, longit. totius $\frac{7}{15}$ adæquans, intus saturate castanea, linea basali albida interrupta; columella pallida, inferne castanea et subacuminate effusa.

Longit. 9 *millim., diam. fere* 6.

Among the shells presented to the British Museum by Mr. Melliss

no such species as *L. helenæ* occurs, nor is it enumerated by Jeffreys
in the list in the 'Annals and Magazine of Natural History.' All
he says concerning it is that it is "a small periwinkle, found abun-
dantly alive and sticking to the rocks all round the sea coast at and
above high-water mark."

I am inclined to believe that the shells which I have associated
with *L. miliaris* are the more common species; but as that was the
only species of this genus received from Mr. Melliss, I have con-
cluded that his *L. helenæ* must be the little conical form described
above.

It is remarkable for its elevated, straight-sided, conical spire, small
aperture, and angular body-whorl. The pale zone on the base is
situated about the middle, so that a small central portion is left of a
rich brown colour. The tubercles on the spire are not closely packed,
but are often separated by spaces wider than themselves.

MODULUS MODULUS, var.

Hab. West Indies generally; Florida for var. *floridana.*

The St. Helena specimens most closely approach that form of this
species which has been named *M. floridanus* by Conrad. None of
them, however, are nearly so large as his figure (Amer. Journ. Conch.
vol. v. pl. xii. fig. 6). The radiating ribs are less numerous and not
so regular; the spotting on the basal ribs, which are finer, is less
distinct, and the concentric furrow near the middle of the base,
which is more conspicuous than the rest, is rather more noticeable.

The considerable variation among the specimens from St. Helena
has induced me to regard them as variations of this American species
rather than as a distinct species. Had they, on the contrary, been
constant in their characters, I believe enough differences might be
indicated to entitle them to specific rank.

PLANAXIS LINEATUS (Da Costa).

Hab. West Indies, St. Vincent's, Jamaica, St. Thomas, St. John's,
St. Martin.

All the specimens from St. Helena are dead shells, and faded, but
seem to belong to this species. It was also obtained at Ascension
Island by Dr. Conry. A very similar species, *Pl. hermannseni,*
Dunker, occurs on the West-African coast at Benguela.

PLANAXIS EBOREUS, Smith.

Hab. St. Thomas and St. Vincent.

The two specimens from St. Helena agree in all respects with
West-Indian examples.

The colouring of the figure of this species (Conch. Icon. vol. xx.
pl. v. fig. 33) is simply absurd. In the copy of the work before me
the entire shell is of a lemon-yellow tint, varied with a few spiral red
lines. All this is imaginary, as the colour is pure white, with the
exception of the brownish apex and the dots on the edge of the
labrum.

LACUNA PUMILIO. (Plate XXIII. fig. 31.)

Testa minuta, albida, late umbilicata, subglobosa, incrementi lineis obliquis striata, aliis spiralibus obsoletis subcancellata ; anfractus tres, convexi, ultimus supra tabulatus et subangulatus, inferne carinis duabus cinctus ; apertura irregulariter ovata, magna, longit. totius ¾ adæquans ; columella fere rectilinearis, anguste reflexa, inferne producta, carinæ umbilicum circumdanti juncta.

Longit. 1½ *millim., diam.* 1½.

Although so small, this does not look like a young shell. Of the two keels on the base of the body-whorl, that bordering the umbilicus is the more conspicuous, and unites with the lower extremity of the columella ; the other runs into the base of the aperture, a little farther off, and the space between is somewhat flat.

FOSSARUS AMBIGUUS (Linné).

Hab. Many parts of the Mediterranean, the coast of Morocco, Cape Verde Islands and Senegal, Madeira and the Canary Islands.

The specimens from St. Helena, which I believe belong to this species, present a very great variation in form. Some closely resemble Adanson's figure (Sénégal, pl. 13. fig. 1), but are rather more widely umbilicated. The majority, however, have the spire scarcely elevated above the body-whorl, the mouth large, and the umbilicus very open, so that, in many cases, the body-whorl is detached from the preceding for a short distance.

The spiral keels, also, are very variable in number and thickness, but all specimens exhibit very much the same kind of fine spiral striæ upon and between the ridges. I see no reason for separating *F. cumingii* of A. Adams from this species; and *F. bicarinatus* of the same author may also be an extreme form of it.

FOSSARUS (COUTHOUYIA) DENTIFER.   (Plate XXIII. fig. 32.)

Testa parva, alba, minute rimata, solida, haud nitens ; anfractus 5–6, apicalis globosus, involutus, cæteri convexi, superne obsolete angulati, lineis incrementi rugosis obliquis striati ; anfr. ultimus magnus, globosus, liris spiralibus distantibus paucis (circiter sex) cinctus ; apertura subcircularis, longit. totius ½ adæquans ; labrum tenue, superne haud sinuatum ; columella arcuata, callosa, infra medium transverse plicata, infra plicam late excavata.

Longit. 2 *millim., diam. max.* 1¾.

The general character of this shell seems to refer it to this genus, but it differs from other species in having a columellar denticle.

The genus *Plicifer* of H. Adams (Proc. Zool. Soc. 1868, p. 293) was founded for a small white shell with a somewhat similar tooth or fold on the pillar. *P. nevilli*, however, has a posterior sinus to the labrum, and differs in other respects from the present species.

FOSSARUS (COUTHOUYIA) LÆVIUSCULUS.   (Plate XXIII. fig. 33.)

Testa parva, anguste umbilicata, ovata, superne acuminata, alba, tenuis; anfractus 5, convexi, microscopice spiraliter striati, sutura subprofunda sejuncti; apertura ovata, superne paulo acuminata, longit. totius ½ subæquans; peristoma tenue, continuum, margine columellari anguste reflexo.

Longit. 3⅛ *millim., diam.* 1⅔.

The spiral striæ are so fine that they can only be seen under a compound microscope. Under a simple lens the surface appears smooth. *Conthouyia plicifera*, A. Adams, has the aperture more distinctly channelled anteriorly, and the umbilicus defined by a carinate margin.

DIALA FUSCOPICTA. (Plate XXI. fig. 20.)

Testa minuta, imperforata, conica, tenuis, nitens, albo-pellucida, strigis fuscis longitudinalibus, et zona interrupta lactea ad peripheriam picta; anfractus 5, vix convexiusculi, primi duo spiraliter tenuiter striati, cæteri læves, ultimus in medio rotunde angulatus; apertura mediocriter magna, longitudinis totius ½ vix æquans; labrum tenue; columella rectiuscula, leviter obliqua, antice subeffusa.

Longit. 2¼ *millim., diam.* 1⅓.

This pretty little shell has the surface smooth, with the exception of the first two whorls, which are finely spirally striated. The upper extremities of the brown stripes do not extend quite to the suture, and on the body-whorl pass between the opaque-white row of dots at the periphery.

RISSOINA MELLISSI. (Plate XXIII. fig. 34.)

Testa ovato-turrita, alba, solidiuscula; anfractus sex, supremi duo convexiusculi, spiraliter striati, cæteris superne tabulati et rotunde angulati, costis validis circiter 11 (in anfr. ultimo ad basim continuis) instructi, striisque spiralibus tenuissimis sculpti; apertura oblique ovata; labrum incrassatum, duplex, superne subsinuatum; margo columellaris callo reflexo, superne labro juncto, indutus.

Longit. 3 *millim., diam.* 1¼.

This is a strongly costate species, with very fine transverse striæ on and between the ribs. The outer basal margin of the aperture has a double lip, and the ribs are more or less regularly continuous up the spire.

RISSOINA TURTONI. (Plate XXIII. fig. 35.)

Testa gracilis, turrita, alba; anfractus 6–7, convexi, sutura obliqua sejuncti, primi duo spiraliter lirati, cæteri costis longitudinalibus 10–12 tenuibus, oblique curvatis, instructi, transversim inter costas tenuissime striati; apertura obliqua, parva, longit. totius ⅓ vix æquans, ad basim late effusa; labrum mediocriter incrassatum, intus longitudinaliter striatum; columella obliqua, parum arcuata.

Longit. 3 *millim., diam.* 1.

The spiral liræ upon the apical whorls are peculiar, and the apex itself is large in proportion to the size of the shell.

RISSOINA DECIPIENS.   (Plate XXIII. fig. 36.)

Testa R. bryeriæ *simillima, sed anfr. ultimo inferne transversim striato, et apertura antice distincte subcanaliculata differt.*
Longit. 4⅓ *millim., diam.* 1½.

This species, unless critically examined, might easily be taken for *P. bryeria.* It differs in having spiral striæ around the lower part of the body-whorl, and the aperture is produced in front into a decided oblique sinus or channel, giving a longer appearance to the mouth. Three specimens of this species were presented to the Museum by E. W. Alexander, Esq., in 1857.

RISSOINA BRYERIA (Montagu).

Turbo bryerius, Montagu, Test. Brit. vol. ii. p. 313, pl. 15. fig. 8.
Rissoina bryeria, Schwartz v. Mohrenstern, Denkschr. k. Akad. Wissensch. Wien, 1861, vol. xix. p. 139, pl. v. fig. 36.

This is a common West-Indian species, and is also said by Schwartz von Mohrenstern to occur at the Mauritius. The two specimens from St. Helena are intermediate in size between average examples of this species and *R. chesneli,* and one of them exhibits a distinct indication of the labral tooth of the latter species (*vide* Schwartz, *l. c.* fig. 39).

No mention of this denticle is made by Michaud, the author of the species; but in the figure given by Schwartz von Mohrensteru, taken from a specimen furnished him by Michaud, it is clearly depicted. This feature and its smaller size alone separate it from *R. bryeria,* and I am inclined, from an examination of a large series of specimens, to believe that neither of these characters are at all reliable, for a perfect gradation in size and in the development of the tooth is observable. I am therefore of opinion that both forms should be regarded in the light of variations of one and the same species.

RISSOINA CONGENITA.   (Plate XXIII. fig. 37.)

Testa R. bryeriæ *similis, sed minor, costis tenuioribus, magis obliquis instructa, inter costas transversim striata; labrum minus incrassatum.*
Longit. 3⅔ *millim., diam.* 1⅓.

The ribs are sharper and more oblique than in *R. bryeria* or the variety *chesneli.* The spiral striation is very fine, and chiefly apparent between the costæ; if, however, the shells were in very fresh condition, it would doubtless pass over the ribs also.

RISSOINA HELENÆ.   (Plate XXIII. fig. 38.)

Testa parva, albida, subpellucida, ovato-turrita ; anfractus 6, duo supremi lævigati, perconvexi, cæteri mediocriter convexi, sutura profunda sejuncti, costis oblique curvatis 15–16 instructi, undique minute spiraliter striati; apex peculiaris, magnus ; apertura obliqua, subpyriformis, longit. totius ⅓ sub-

20*

*æquans; columella basi incrassata producta; labrum incras-
satum.*
Longit. 2⅔ *millim., diam.* 1.
The apex of this species is very peculiar, being large, smooth, and
somewhat uncoiled.

Rissoa cala. (Plate XXI. fig. 21.)

*Testa ovato-pyramidalis, nitida, mediocriter tenuis, albida,
lineis vel strigis longitudinalibus undulatis irregularibus
picta; anfractus 6, leviter convexi, lævigati; apex subacutus,
spiraliter tenuissime striatus; anfract. ultimus ad basim
albus, haud variegatus, in medio obsolete rotunde subangulatus;
apertura rotundata, intus albida; columella fusco tincta;
labrum tenue, album.*
Longit. 3 *millim., diam.* 1½.
The brownish markings are irregular in shape and direction, and
give most of the specimens the appearance of being mottled with
brown and white. Some examples, however, which have only a
brownish zone round the middle of the body-whorl, bear considerable resemblance to *Barleeia rubra*, Montagu. That species has
not the same spiral striation on the upper volutions.

Rissoa epiiamilla. (Plate XXI. fig. 22.)

*Testa ovato-pyramidalis, lævigata, albida, infra suturam opaco-
albo et rufo-fusco maculata; anfract. 6, vix convexi, ultimus
ad basim lineis radiantibus fuscis ornatus; apertura rotundata, longit. totius ⅓ subæquans; columella fusco-purpureo
tincta; labrum vix incrassatum.*
Longit. 4 *millim., diam.* 2.
This species must not be confused with *R. cala.* It is a little
larger, somewhat more solid, has rather less convex whorls, and is
not coloured in the same way. Both have the columella stained
with a brown or purplish-brown colour, and united to the outer lip
above by a thin callus.

Rissoa glypta. (Plate XXIII. fig. 39.)

*Testa ovato-pyramidalis, alba vel rufescens, imperforata, nitida;
anfractus 6, apicales læves, convexi, cæteri superne declives,
interdum paulo excavati, in medio aut obtuse vel subacute
angulati, infra angulum contracti, liris spiralibus tenuibus
cincti, interdum ad angulum plus minus longitudinaliter
plicati; apertura rotunde ovata, longit. totius ⅓ adæquans,
peristoma continuum, margine basali subeffuso, columellari
anguste reflexo.*
Longit. 3½ *millim., diam.* 1½.
In some specimens the walls are much more angular than in
others, and the longitudinal plicæ vary also very much in
development.

Rissoa eritima.   (Plate XXIII. fig. 40.)

Testa ovata, umbilicata, albo-pellucida, nitida; anfractus 4, sutura profunda discreti, convexi, duo supremi lævis, cæteri striis spiralibus tenuissimis sculpti, ultimus magnus, sub-globosus; umbilicus falciformis, in medio lira tenuissima instructus; apertura rotunde ovata, superne acuminata, longit. totius ½ æquans; peristoma continuum, vix incrassatum, ad basim columellæ subeffusum vel indistincte sub-canaliculatum.

Longit. 1⅔ *millim., diam.* 1.

This is more widely umbilicated than *R. soluta*, Philippi, is more regularly spirally striated, has a slight indication of a sinus at the base of the columella, and also differs in other particulars.

Rissoa agapeta.   (Plate XXI. fig. 23.)

Testa ovata, imperforata, nitida, subpellucida, lineis spiralibus fuscis interruptis ornata; anfractus 5, convexi, duo supremi minutissime subpunctati, cæteri spiraliter sulcati, sutura profunda sejuncti; apertura ovata, superne leviter acuminata, longit. totius ½ haud æquans; peristoma tenue, margine columellari anguste reflexo, superne labro callo tenui juncto.

Longit. 1⅔ *millim., diam. fere* 1.

The microscopic sculpture of the apical whorls has a very pretty shagreened appearance. The spiral sulci are about five in number on the penultimate volution, and twelve on the last. The uninterrupted brown lines fall on the ridges between the grooves. *R. depicta*, Manzoni, from Madeira, is an allied but larger form.

Rissoa compsa.   (Plate XXIII. fig. 41.)

Testa ovata, inperforata, parum nitida, albida vel dilute fus-cescens; anfractus 5, convexi, sutura profunda discreti, sulcis spiralibus fortibus (in anfr. penult. circiter 5, in ultimo ad 12) sculpti; apertura rotunde ovata, superne leviter acuminata, longit. totius ½ haud æquans; peristoma continuum, vix incrassatum, ad basim obsolete expansum.

Longit. 2 *millim., diam.* 1.

When placed side by side, this species is seen to be a trifle larger than *R. agapeta*, and a little smaller than *R. depicta*. It also differs from both in colour, and is more strongly grooved than either.

Rissoa wallichi.   (Plate XXI. fig. 24.)

Testa ovata, solida, alba, interdum zona rufa cincta, imperforata; anfractus 5–6, primi duo spiraliter tenuiter striati, cæteri plani-usculi, carinis volventibus prominentibus (in anfr. superioribus tribus, in ultimo 7–8) instructi, sutura profunda sejuncti; apertura ovata, longit. totius ⅓ paulo superans; peristoma continuum, margine externo leviter incrassato, columellari antice subdilatato.

Longit. 3 *millim., diam.* 1½.

The red zone, when present, occupies the central part of the last

volution and the lower portion of the upper whorls; it is often
dotted with white.

RISSOA PERFECTA.   (Plate XXIII. fig. 42.)

Testa brevis, ovata, nitida, pellucida, cornea, supra carinas rufo vel
fusco punctata, imperforata; anfractus 4, primus lævis, cæteri
superne tabulati, carinis fortibus (in anfr. superioribus 2,
ultimo 5) instructi, sutura marginata discreti; apertura oblique
rotundo-ovata, longit. totius ⅔ haud æquans; peristoma con-
tinuum, margine externo extus incrassato. columellari leviter
reflexo.
Longit. 2 millim., diam. 1.

This charming little species is at once recognizable by the strong
red-dotted spiral ridges. The dots usually fall under one another,
forming longitudinal series.

RISSOA VARICIFERA.   (Plate XXIV. figs. 1, 1 *a*.)

Testa ovato-acuminata, imperforata, alba, flavescens vel rufescens;
anfractus 5, supremi duo convexi, tenuiter spiraliter lirati,
sequentes convexiusculi, sutura profunda sejuncti, carinis spira-
libus (in anfr. superioribus 3, in ultimo 7–8) instructi; striis mi-
croscopicis spiralibus sculpti; apertura parva, ovata, longit. totius
⅓ adæquans; peristoma continuum, margine externo tenui,
varice valido paulo remoto instructo, columellari obliquo, anguste
reflexo.
Longit. 1¾ millim., diam. ¾.

The little varix at a short distance from the extreme thin edge of
the labrum is of a convex swollen character. A series of specimens
from Madeira, presented to the British Museum by the Rev. R. Boog
Watson, very closely approach this species; they are referred to by
him (Proc. Zool. Soc. 1873, p. 374) under the name *R. subcarinata.*

RISSOA PSEUSTES.   (Plate XXIV. fig. 2.)

Testa ovata, subrimata, tennis, fuscescenti-cornea, nitida, pellucida;
anfractus 4, convexi, duo apicales striis microscopicis spiralibus
striati, cæteri fere læves, infra suturam rufescentes, distincte
marginati; apertura ovata, postice angustata, longit. totius ⅓
paulo minor; peristoma tenue, continuum. margine columellari
rufescente, anguste reflexo.
Longit. 1⅓ millim., diam. ¾.

This minute species, of which there are four specimens, has
rather the look of an embryonic shell. It may prove to be a
Jeffreysia. It is very like *R. perminima*, Watson (? not of Manzoni),
Proc. Zool. Soc. 1873. p. 383, but seems rather shorter and has no
basal striæ.

BARLEEIA CONGENITA   (Plate XXI. fig. 25.)

Testa solida, obtuse ovato-conoidalis, lævis, saturate rufa, infra
suturam albo marginata vel maculata, infra medium anfract.
ultimi alba; anfr. 5, convexiusculi, ultimus ad peripheriam
obtuse rotunde angulatus; apertura rotundata, superne leviter

acuminata, intus rufescens; columella reflexa, fusco tincta, superne labro juncta ; labrum vix incrassatum, pallidum. Longit. 2½ *millim., diam. fere* 1½.

This species is considerably like *B. rubra* of the British coast. It is, however, of a stumpier form, the spire being less produced, and the body-whorl longer in proportion to the spire.

CÆCUM JUCUNDUM, de Folin.

C. jucundum, de Folin, Fonds de la Mer, vol. i. p. 20, pl. 2. figs. 6, 7.

Hab. Guadeloupe.

CÆCUM IMBRICATUM, Carpenter.

Cæcum imbricatum, Carp. Proc. Zool. Soc. 1858, p. 422.

Hab. West Indies.

CÆCUM (MEIOCERAS) NITIDUM, Bean.

Meioceras nitidum (Bean), Carp. P. Z. S. 1858, p. 438.

Hab. W. Indies.

CERITHIUM (BITTIUM) GIBBERULUM, var.

Cerithium gibberulum, C. B. Adams Proc. Bost. Soc. N. Hist. 1845, vol. ii. p. 5 ; Sowerby, Thes. Conch. vol. ii. p. 876, pl. 184. figs. 210, 211 ; id. Reeve's Conch. Icon. pl. 18. fig. 123.

Hab. Jamaica.

The specimens from St. Helena are much paler than those from the West Indies. The varix on the back of the body-whorl is whitish in all, and usually has some short brown lines on the transverse liræ behind it, and a dark brown spot in front.

TRIFORIS PERVERSA (Linné).

Hab. Mediterranean, North Sea, English Channel, Atlantic coasts of France and Portugal, North-west Africa and Madeira, Canary Islands and the Azores.

The specimens from St. Helena are as variable in form as those from other localities, some being very much more slender than others. The minute bead-like granules are pale in colour, and contrast strongly with the rich brown dots between them. The central row of granules on the penultimate and preceding volutions is almost as large as the others in the majority of the specimens.

TRIFORIS MELANURA (C. B. Adams).

Cerithium melanura, C. B. Adams, Contrib. Conchol. p. 117.

Hab. Jamaica.

A few specimens of a whitish colour, with the exception of the four apical whorls and the cauda of the last, which are brown, possibly belong to this species. For the most part, however, they have the central spiral series of granules on the penultimate and one or two preceding whorls rather finer than the others. In other respects they accord with Adams's description.

TRIFORIS ATLANTICA.   (Plate XXI. fig. 26.)

*Testa haud perelongata, alba, livido-fusco inferne zonata; anfrac-
tus 13, anguste turriti, supremi minute cancellati, cæteri plani,
granulorum seriebus duobus vel tribus cincti, ultimus seriebus
quinque, infima minus tuberculata, ornatus; cauda brevis,
carina valida instructa, fuscescens; apertura obliqua, ovata,
superne canaliculata; peristoma superne leviter incisum, inferne
columellæ callo crasso junctum.*

Longit. 6 *millim., diam.* 2.

The outlines of this species are a little convex. Only the penultimate and antepenultimate whorls have three distinct rows of
granules, and of those the central one is the smallest. The granules
of the lowermost series, or rather the interstices between them, are
brown and the uppermost series is white.

TRIFORIS RECTA.   (Plate XXIV. fig. 3.)

*Testa elongata, gracilis, fuscescens, ad apicem plerumque pallida;
anfractus 13, primi duo bicarinati, cæteri liris tribus, granosis,
subæqualibus, cincti, ultimus liris duabus simplicibus infra
medium instructus; linea suturalis canaliculata; apertura
parva, ovalis; labrum superne leviter sinuatum; columella callo
incrassato induta: canalis brevissimus, haud clausus.*

Longit. 5 *millim., diam.* 1¼.

This species is more slender than any of the others from
St. Helena, and remarkable on account of the sculpture of the apical
whorls, which is not fine as in *T. melanura* and *T. perversa*, but
consists of two strong spiral keels on each whorl. The above-
mentioned species also have only two series of granules on the whorls
towards the apex, whereas in the present species there are three.

TRIFORIS BATHYRAPHE.   (Plate XXIV. fig. 4.)

*Testa haud perelongata, albida vel pallide fusca; anfractus 11,
convexiusculi, sutura profunda sejuncti, liris spiralibus tribus
subæqualibus, lirisque longitudinalibus circiter 26 granose cancellati; anfr. ultimus liris sexcinctus; apertura rotunde ovata;
labrum tenue, superne ad suturam anguste sinuatum, inferne
columellæ junctum; cauda brevis, leviter recurva.*

Longit. 5¾ *millim., diam.* 2.

This species is peculiar on account of the deep suture and the
distinct cancellation of the surface. The whorls, too, are convex, so
that the central row of granules are most prominent. It is a much
stouter shell than *T. recta* and has a different aperture.

CERITHIOPSIS RUGULOSA (C. B. Adams).

Cerithium rugulosum, C. B. Adams, Contributions to Conch.
p. 121; Sowerby, Thes. Conch. pl. 184. fig. 237 (237 * ?).

Hab. Jamaica (*Adams*); St. Vincent's (*Brit. Mus.*); Algiers
(*Sowerby*)?

In the Cumingian Collection there is a single specimen of this species and one of *C. vicinum*, which were received from Adams himself. On examination they seem to me to belong to one and the same species, the difference in thickness of the spiral and transverse ridges being very slight. Some of the St. Helena examples exceed the dimensions given by the author, having a length of 6 millimetres, and they consist of ten normal and three nuclear whorls. The slightly elevated spiral line mentioned by Adams is at the top of the whorls just below the suture, and the "*fourth*" spiral nodulous slender ridge on the body-whorl should have been termed the *fifth*.

CERITHIOPSIS NEGLECTA (C. B. Adams).

Cerithium neglectum, C. B. Adams, Panama Shells, p. 154.

Hab. Panama (*Adams*); Algiers (*Sowerby*).

This is a minute dark brown granulated shell, consisting of about twelve whorls, of which the three or four apical are transparent, glossy, smooth, and separated by a brown sutural line. Adams observes that there are two additional spiral ridges on the lower part of the body-whorl, whereas I distinctly count three, both in Panama and St. Helena specimens. With this exception, no fault can be found with his diagnosis. Sowerby's figures (Thesaurus Conch. pl. 184. figs. 235, 236) either represent another species, as each whorl has but two rows of granules, or else have been carelessly drawn.

HIPPONYX ANTIQUATUS (Linné).

Hab. West Indies, Fernando Noronha, island of Trinidad in the South Atlantic, and Ascension Island; Loanda (*Dunker*).

HIPPONYX GRAYANUS, Menke.

Hab. West coast of Central America, Sandwich Islands, Fernando Noronha.

I have given the distribution of this and the preceding species, also references and synonymy, in my account of the Mollusca of Fernando Noronha, which will be published in the Journal of the Linnean Society.

TEINOSTOMA ? ABNORME.   (Plate XXIV. fig. 5.)

Testa minuta, alba, pellucida, subglobosa, imperforata; anfractus 3, rapide accrescentes, sutura canaliculata sejuncti; anfract. ultimus magnus, minute spiraliter striatus, in regione umbilicali callo crasso instructus; spira plana, haud elevata; apertura magna, ovata, inferne effusa; columella arcuata, callo crasso reflexo induta.

Longit. 1 millim., *diam. max.* 1.

Although so minute, the above measurements probably represent the adult size of this species. It does not agree with the typical forms of *Teinostoma* in the shape of the aperture; but in texture and colour it is very similar.

TURBO (COLLONIA) RUBRICINCTUS, Mighels, var.

Turbo rubricinctus, Mighels, Proc. Bost. Soc. Nat. Hist. 1845, vol. ii. p. 22.

Leptothyra rubrilineata, Garrett; Martens, Donnm Bismarki-anum, p. 48, pl. ii. fig. 15.

Turbo (Collonia) rubricinctus, Sowerby, Thes. Conch. vol. v. p. 212, pl. 13. fig. 157.

Collonia rubrilineata, Pease, MS., Sowerby, *l. c.*

Collonia multistriata, Pease, MS., Sowerby, *l. c.*

Hab. Sandwich Islands.

None of the specimens from the Sandwich Islands, which I have seen, appear to be quite as large as those from St. Helena. The former have a rosy apex to the spire, whilst in the latter it is pale. Dr. von Martens (Don. Bism. p. 48) considers this species the same as *Collonia verruca*, Gould. The difference in size and colour at once distinguishes them. Some of the St. Helena specimens are coloured like the type-forms, whilst others are reddish brown, with a few pale interruptions on the spiral ridges.

TURBO (COLLONIA) ADMISSUS. (Plate XXII. fig. 4.)

Testa minuta, anguste umbilicata, conico-globosa, alba, radiatim rufo-fusco lineata vel flammulata, punctis rufis minutis tessellata; anfractus 5, superne declives, dein angulati, ad angulum carinati, liris tenuibus paucis cincti, ultimus infra medium subangulatus, carina circa umbilicum instructus; apertura subrotundata, longit. totius ½ adæquans; columella arcuata, alba, leviter reflexa.

Longit. 2½ *millim., diam. maj.* 2.

The generic position of this pretty minute species is at present somewhat uncertain, as the operculum is unknown. On account of its small size and non-nacreous interior, I believe it to belong to *Collonia*. One specimen is of a pinkish tint, and all show a more or less distinct darkish zone on the lower surface of the body-whorl. The minute dots fall upon the fine spiral liræ.

PHASIANELLA TESSELLATA, C. B. Adams.

Phasianella tessellata, C. B. Adams, Contrib. Conch. p. 67.

Hab. Jamaica.

The coloration of this species is variable, but the "fine, rather distant, parallel, spiral lines of brown, which descend more rapidly than the whorls," appear to be quite constant. In young fresh specimens more or less spiral striation is discernible.

LIOTIA ARENULA. (Plate XXIV. fig. 6.)

Testa minuta, depresse globosa, anguste umbilicata, alba; an-fractus 3–3½, superne subplani, in medio rotunde angulati, microscopice spiraliter striati, radiatim plicati, transversim-que lirati, ultimus carinis vel liris spiralibus sex, lirisque obliquis numerosis cancellatus; sutura profunda, canalicu-

lata; apertura rotundata; peristoma leviter incrassatum, marginibus continuis, dextro subpatulo.
Longit. ½ millim., diam. maj. 1⅛.

The beauty of this species can only be seen under the microscope. The cancellation of the body-whorl is strongly developed, so that the pittings between the cross-ridges are deep and striking. The uppermost of the six revolving liræ borders the channelled suture, and the umbilicus is encompassed by a swollen ridge, which is in addition to the six liræ referred to. The microscopic striæ are seen upon the liræ.

LIOTIA ADMIRABILIS.   (Plate XXIV. fig. 7.)

Testa minuta, profunde umbilicata, depresse globosa, alba; an- fractus 3½, superne declives, planulati, in medio angulati, infra angulum plani, cancellati, ultimus carinis transversis quinque, lamellis longitudinalibus paulo obliquis circiter 16 instructus; apertura circularis; peristoma incrassatum, con- tinuum, marginibus callo tenui junctis.
Longit. 1 *millim., diam. maj.* 1⅓.

This very minute species is a strongly sculptured shell like *L. asteriscus*, Gould, and *L. speciosa*, Angas. It is, however, much smaller than either.

The uppermost of the keels on the body-whorl revolves up the spire and forms the angle on the upper volutions; the lowermost carina borders the umbilicus, and the next occupies the middle of the under surface. The longitudinal lamellæ are continuous on and between the keels.

GENA ASPERULATA, A. Adams.

Gena asperulata, A. Adams, Proc. Zool. Soc. 1850, p. 38; Thes. Conch. vol. ii. p. 831, pl. 173. figs. 28, 29; Sowerby, Conch. Icon. pl. ii. fig. 16.

Hab.—? (*Adams*): St. Thomas (*Brit. Mus.*).

The colour of this species is very variable. Some specimens are pink, tessellated with white; others are olive-brown with white spots; some have few spots, others many. None of the St. Helena shells are marked like the type, but they agree with it in form and sculpture, which is peculiar, and in having the apex of the spire white.

EMARGINULA ELONGATA, Costa.

Hab. Mediterranean.

A single small specimen, 5 millim. in length, apparently belongs to this species. The cancellation of its surface is, however, a little finer than usual. *E. maculata*, A. Adams, from Japan, also closely resembles this specimen in form and sculpture.

FISSURELLA GIBBERULA, Lamarck?

Several specimens, the largest of which is hardly ten millim. long, appear to belong to this species. *F. variegata*, Sow., and

F. arcuata, Sow., may also be forms of it. The distribution and synonymy is given by Weinkauff (Conch. Mittelm. vol. ii. p. 394). The specimens collected by Mr. Melliss were named *F. arcuata*, Sow., by Jeffreys[1], but in sculpture they more nearly resemble the typical form of *F. gibberula*. In *F. arcuata* the costæ are very closely approximated to one another. Young specimens, in which the capuliform apex has not been absorbed, have the appearance of the genus *Puncturella*.

PATELLA PLUMBEA, Lamarck.

Patella plumbea, Reeve, Conch. Icon. pl. iii. figs. 5 *a–b*.
Patella cærulea, Quoy & Gaimard, Voy. Astrolabe, Moll. vol. iii. p. 342, pl. 70. figs. 4–6.
Patella cyanea, Lesson, Voy. Coquille, vol. ii. p. 417.
Patella canescens, Reeve, *op. cit.* pl. 34. figs. 103 *a–b*.
Hab. St. Helena (*Q. & G.*, *Lesson*); Senegal (*Lamarck*).

If, as I am inclined to believe, *P. canescens* be a variety of this species, it shows that it is a very variable form. A considerable number of very young shells were collected by Capt. Turton, which probably are the early stages of different varieties of this species. They are extremely variable in colour, but it is impossible to distinguish them on that account alone.

WILLIAMIA GUSSONII (Costa).

Ancylus gussonii, Costa, Cat. Test. due Sicil. pp. 120 & 125.
Patella pellucida, Philippi, Moll. Sicil. vol. i. p. 111, pl. 7. fig. 7.
Patella gussonii, id. l. c. p. 255, vol. ii. p. 84.
Patella radiata, Pease, Proc. Zool. Soc. 1860, p. 437.
Hab. Some parts of the Mediterranean, Madeira, Canary Islands, Ascension Island.

The specimens from St. Helena and Ascension Island are precisely similar, and agree exactly with the shells in Cuming's collection marked *Patella radiata*, Pease, and which, I presume, are the types described, and supposed to have come from the Sandwich Islands. Examples from the Canaries have the apex more excentric than the majority of St. Helena specimens, and they are less distinctly rayed. The radiating ribs mentioned by Pease are very indistinct. In his list of shells collected by Mr. Melliss at St. Helena (Ann. Mag. Nat. Hist. 1872, vol. ix. p. 264) Jeffreys has quoted this species under the name of *Tectura virginea*, Müller. The latter species, however, I believe is quite distinct.

BULLA STRIATA, Bruguière.

Hab. Mediterranean, West Indies, Brazil, West Africa.

With this species I unite *B. media* and *B. adansonii*, Philippi, respectively from the West Indies and West Africa. I do not think the slight differences pointed out by Philippi possess more than varietal value. I have seen specimens from both localities with the superior as well as the inferior striæ.

[1] Ann. & Mag. Nat. Hist. 1872, vol. ix. p. 264.

CYLICHNA CYLINDRACEA (Pennant).

Hab. This species occurs throughout " the whole north-east Atlantic, from the Lofotens to the Mediterranean, at the Canaries and Mogador " (*Watson*). It was also obtained by the 'Challenger' at Ascension Island and Tristan da Cunha, and the British Museum possesses specimens collected at Whydah on the west coast of Africa. Several of the specimens belong to the variety "*linearis*" (Jeffreys, Brit. Conch. vol. iv. p. 416).

CYLICHNA ATLANTICA.   (Plate XXIV. fig. 10.)

Testa ovato-cylindracea, tenuis, pellucido-alba, nitens, rimata, ad verticem anguste perforata, transversim (praesertim supra et infra) tenuissime striata; apertura superne angustissima, antice leviter dilatata; labrum tenue, supra verticem anfr. ultimi productum; margo columellaris callo tenui reflexo indutus, inferne obsolete subtruncatum.

Longit. 5½ *millim., diam.* 2¼.

This species has more curved outlines than *C. cylindracea*, has a perforate apex, and an umbilical chink. The thin columellar callosity extends up the whorl, and joins the upper extremity of the outer lip.

CYLICHNA BIDENTATA (d'Orbigny.)

Bulla bidentata, d'Orbigny, Sagra's Hist. Cuba, Moll. vol. i. p. 125, pl. 4. figs. 13–16.

Hab. West Indies.

The specimens from St. Helena agree in all respects with this species, except that the lower columellar tooth, or fold, is less developed. Similar variation occasionally occurs in West-Indian examples.

TORNATINA RECTA (d'Orbigny).

Bulla recta, d'Orbigny, Sagra's Hist. Cuba, vol. i. p. 131, pl. 4 bis. figs. 17–20.

Hab. West Indies.

A single specimen is all I have seen from St. Helena. It has the spire rather less elevated than d'Orbigny's type.

PHILINE QUADRATA, Searles Wood.

Hab. North Britain, Norway, Greenland, Massachusetts Bay, Azores.

A single specimen was dredged in 50–80 fathoms. It has the transverse sculpture rather finer than usual.

HAMINEA HYDATIS (Linné).

Hab. British Coast, Mediterranean, &c.

None of the specimens from St. Helena exceed 10 millim. in length; they therefore are probably not full-grown.

ACTÆON SEMISCULPTUS. (Plate XXIV. fig. 8.)

Testa ovata, turrita, parva, nitida, nivea, angustissime rimata, superne lævis, infra medium subdilstanter transversim punctato-striata ad basim confertius striata, sulcis paucis longitudinalibus indistinctis, crenatis, distantibus sculpta ; anfractus quatuor, leviter convexi, sutura anguste canaliculata sejuncti ; apex invo-lutus ; apertura inverse auriformis, longit. totius ½ paullo superans ; columella anguste reflexa, plica parva prope rimam munita.

Longit. 4 millim., diam. 2¼

The spiral transverse punctured striæ do not extend above the middle of the body-whorl. The longitudinal narrow and shallow indistinct sulci apparently indicate lines of growth.

LEUCOTINA MINUTA. (Plate XXIV. fig. 9.)

Testa minuta, oblonga, alba ; anfractus 5, primus (nucleus) rotun-datus, introversus, spiraliter liratus, cæteri convexi, liris tenui-bus spiralibus (in anfr. penult. circiter 7) instructi, in interstitiis, liris paulo angustioribus, lineis longitudinalibus tenuissimis sculpti ; apertura ovata, superne acuminata, inferne cum colu-mella arcuata et dilatata leviter effusa ; plica columellæ centralis, distincta.

Longit. 2¼ millim., diam. ¾. Var. brevior 2¼ longa, 1 lata.

The apex of this interesting species is peculiar, being introverted as it were, and partly enveloped by the succeeding whorl. It is not smooth, as is frequently the case in other species, but obliquely spirally lirate. The raised lines in the grooves between the ridges produce a subpunctate appearance.

The genera *Myonia* and *Leucotina* were described by A. Adams in the 'Annals and Magazine of Natural History,' 1860, vol. v. p. 406. On examining the diagnoses a great similarity is observ-able, and, indeed, with the exception of a slight difference in form, there seems to be very little, if any, distinction. I therefore would propose that these genera be united, in which case *Leucotina* may be retained, *Myonia* being preoccupied. *M. japonica,* A. Adams, I have not seen ; but *Actæon modesta,* A. Adams, *Monoptygma casta* = *M. concinna,* both of A. Adams, and *Daphnella casta,* Hinds, all typical forms of *Myonia,* have been examined, and they do not offer any characters which will separate them generically from *Leucotina niphonensis,* A. Adams, *L. dianæ,* A. Adams (described as an *Actæon*), &c.

One of the species of this genus, *L. casta,* A. Adams, has been referred by Watson (' Challenger' Report of Gasteropoda, p. 487) to the section *Parthenia* of *Odostomia* ; but this location is not cor-rect, I think—*Parthenia*[1], comprising longitudinally-ribbed shells, being apparently synonymous with *Chemnitzia,* d'Orbigny, or *Tur-bonilla,* Risso, 1826. Judging from the shell-characters, I should

[1] This name was proposed by Lowe in 1840. It had previously (1830) been used by Robineau-Desvoidy for a genus of Insects.

be inclined to place this form in the *Actæonidæ*, as recommended by Adams, rather than in the *Pyramidellidæ*.

Some confusion appears to exist with regard to the genus *Monoptygma*, judging from the variety of shells which have been placed in it. The original type described by Lea under the name of *M. alabamensis* is a fossil, and evidently allied to *Ancillaria*, with which it is associated both by Tryon and Fischer in their recent Manuals. A. Adams published a monograph of this genus in the 'Proceedings of the Zoological Society' for 1851 (reproduced in Sowerby's 'Thesaurus Conchyliorum,' vol. ii.), including in it a number of species, none of which, in fact, have any relationship with *Monoptygma*. He subsequently removed all of these species to other genera, with the exception of *M. striatum* and *M. fulvum*. A species very closely allied to these forms has since been described by Lischke from Japan, under the name of *M. eximium*. As far as I can ascertain, no generic or subgeneric division has been proposed for these species. If as much latitude in variation of form be allowed in the genus *Leucotina* as in some other genera (e. g., *Murex, Triton, Mitra*, &c.), there is no occasion to establish a new division for these three and allied species, for, with the exception of being more elongate than typical species of the genus, they do not offer any material differences in regard to the aperture, sculpture, or the apical whorls.

UMBRELLA MEDITERRANEA, Lamarck?

This well-known Mediterranean shell also occurs at Madeira and the Cape de Verde Islands, but it has not previously been recorded from so southern a locality as St. Helena. Krauss[1] quotes *U. indica* as a Cape species, so that I am uncertain whether the two young shells from St. Helena should not be referred to that species, if in reality it is distinct from the Mediterranean form. It is stated by Eydoux and Souleyet, in the 'Zoology of the Bonite,' that the animals do not differ, and, as far as I have studied the shells, the two typical forms appear to pass one into the other.

TYLODINA CITRINA, Joannis.

Tylodina citrina, Joannis, Mag. de Zool. 1834, pl. 36; Grube, Ausflug Triest und Quarnero, pp. 58 & 120.

Hab. Mediterranean (*Joannis, Grube, Monterosato, &c.*); Canary Islands (*McAndrew, teste Weinkauff*).

Only some small specimens, about 7 millim. in length, were obtained. They agree in every particular with the apical portion of large Mediterranean examples with which I have compared them. The minute nucleus consists of about two spirally-coiled whorls, is glossy, vitreous, and laterally inclined.

[1] Südafr. Moll. p. 62.

PEDIPES AFER (Gmelin).

Hab. Portugal, Azores, Madeira, Salvages, and some parts of the shore of West Africa.

This well-known species has not been previously recorded from St. Helena. None of the specimens obtained by Capt. Turton were living, but were found in the hard kind of conglomerate of shells and sand mentioned in the introductory observations.

GADINIA COSTATA (Krauss).

Mouretia costata, Krauss, Südafr. Moll. p. 57, pl. 4. fig. 1.
Gadinia costata, Dall, Amer. Journ. Conch. vol. vi. p. 11.
Hab. Cape of Good Hope.

The St. Helena specimens have more colour than most of the South African shells I have seen. In other respects they are similar.

The following HETEROPODA were obtained by dredging :—

OXYGYRUS KERAUDRENII, Lesueur.

ATLANTA PERONII, Lesueur.

ATLANTA INCLINATA, Eydoux & Souleyet.

The synonymy and distribution of these species are given in my Report on the ' Challenger ' Heteropoda.

IV. SCAPHOPODA.

CADULUS JEFFREYSII, Monterosato.

The synonymy and distribution of this species are given by Jeffreys (Proc. Zool. Soc. 1882, p. 665). I have carefully compared the series of specimens from St. Helena with others obtained by the ' Porcupine ' Expedition in the Atlantic, and can find no difference, except in size. Those from St. Helena are a trifle smaller.

V. PELECYPODA.

VENUS (VENTRICOLA) EFFOSSA, Bivona.

Venus effossa, Bivona, Pfeiffer, Conch.-Cab. p. 197, pl. 32. figs. 1–4.

Hab. Sicily, Naples, Corsica, Algeria, Canary Islands, Azores.

The largest of the specimens from St. Helena is twenty-five millimetres long and high, and twenty-three in diameter. None of them have the lunule quite as deep as the Mediterranean shells figured by Pfeiffer and Philippi (Moll. Sicil. vol. i. pl. iii. fig. 20). *V. toreuma*, Gould, is very closely related to this species, but may be distinguished by its finer concentric ribs, which are more or less granular. *V. effossa* is radiately striated, especially at the anterior and posterior ends. The colour of the specimens at hand is similar to the above-cited figure in the ' Conchylien-Cabinet.'

VENUS (CHIONE) PYGMÆA, Lamarck.

Venus pygmæa, Lamarck, An. s. Vert. ed. 2, vol. vi. p. 337; Hanley,
Cat. Recent Shells, p. 110, pl. 16. fig. 13; Sowerby, Thes. Con.
vol. ii. p. 707, pl. 156. figs. 69–72; Reeve, Con. Icon. pl. 26.
fig. 138 *a–c*.

Hab. West Indies.

Of this well-defined species I have seen only a single specimen
from St. Helena. It is not rayed with pink, as is frequently the
case, but merely presents a few brown spots, disposed in rays upon
a whitish ground, and a few cross-lines on the excavated hinder
dorsal area.

CYTHEREA (CARYATIS) RUDIS (Poli).

Cytherea rudis, Pfeiffer, Conch.-Cab. p. 34, pl. 11. figs. 9, 10.

Hab. Mediterranean, Adriatic and Black Seas, Canary Islands.

The shells from St. Helena are rather strongly concentrically
sculptured. The largest is 22 millim. in length, and none have a
coloured lunule.

TELLINA ANTONII, Philippi.

Hab. Guadaloupe, West Indies.

As far as I can ascertain the above is the only locality quoted for
this species. In the British Museum "East Africa" and "Amboyna" are attached to some specimens which undoubtedly belong
to this species; but I regard both with suspicion. The three valves
from St. Helena are long and narrow, being 55 millim. in length and
23 in height. They agree in form with *T. cumingii*, as figured in
Reeve's 'Conchologia Iconica,' fig. 179 *a*, and, indeed, I question if
the limits of that and the present species can be clearly defined.

The *form* is subject to considerable variation, even among specimens which have identical sculpture, some being much narrower
than others. The radiating striæ also differ much in development,
and although their presence in *T. cumingii* is not mentioned by
Hanley, they have been detected by Römer; and in all the specimens which I have examined their presence, especially in the right
valve, is undeniable. *T. cumingii* has been recorded from the west
coast of Central America by Hanley, C. B. Adams, and others, so it
may be presumed that that is its true locality, and *not* the Red Sea,
quoted by Sowerby in the 'Conchologia Iconica.'

SEMELE CORDIFORMIS (Chemnitz).

Tellina cordiformis, Chemn. Conch.-Cab. vol. xi. figs. 1941–2.
Amphidesma cordiformis, Reeve, Conch. Icon. pl. 5. fig. 30.

Hab. West Indies, Georgia, Florida, Brazil, West Africa, West
Colombia.

With this species I unite *Amphidesma orbiculata* and *A. radiata*,
both of Say, *A. subtruncata*, Sowerby, *A. reticulata*, Sowerby, *A.*
decussata, Wood, *A. luteola*, A. Adams, *A. lenticularis*, Sowerby,
and *A. modesta*, A. Adams. I believe these so-called species merely

represent varieties and different stages of the same shell. The locality " Indian Ocean " given by Reeve to *Am. cordiformis*, which he assigns to Sowerby, is evidently incorrect. Say's species were from Georgia and E. Florida, *A. reticulata,* *subtruncata,* and *decussata* from the West Indies, *A. lenticularis* from West Colombia, and *A. modesta* from West Africa.

The shells from St. Helena are only young specimens, 18 millim. in length, and agree with *A. modesta* as figured by Reeve (Conch. Icon. fig. 35 *b*).

ERVILIA SUBCANCELLATA, Smith.

Ervilia subcancellata, Smith, ' Challenger ' Lamellibr. p. 80, pl. vi. figs. 2–2 *b*.

Hab. West Indies; Fernando Noronha ; Brazil ; 25–675 fathoms.

The concentric sculpture is much coarser in some specimens than in others, and the radiating striæ, as formerly pointed out, also vary. Young specimens, which are pellucid, exhibit on each side towards the end of the dorsal margin a small brown spot, also occasionally observable in more adult shells.

CORBULA SWIFTIANA, C. B. Adams.

Corbula swiftiana, C. B. Adams, Contrib. Conch. p. 236.

Hab. Jamaica, St. Thomas, Hayti.

CARDIUM (FRAGUM) SPECIOSUM, Adams & Reeve.

Cardium speciosum, Adams & Reeve, Voy. 'Samarang,' p. 77, pl. xxii. fig. 9.

Hab. China Sea (*Ad. & Rve.*).

After a very careful comparison of the St. Helena specimens with the type of this species preserved in the British Museum, I have no hesitation in pronouncing them one and the same form. In shape and sculpture they are identical, but differ in having about three more ribs. The locality assigned to this species is possibly, or probably, erroneous, and I think it likely it may have been obtained at St. Helena on the voyage home, for, as stated by Mr. Adams in the preface to the ' Voyage,' p. vi, the ' Samarang' touched at St. Helena. Whether this species should or should not be regarded merely as a variety of the West-Indian *C. medium,* Linné, I cannot now determine, not having a sufficient series of either for studying their variation or constancy. *C. medium,* however, has a less oblique form, and seems to be a broader shell, or, in other words, has a longer ventral margin, which is not so obliquely upsloping in front. The ribs, too, are usually flatter, and sculptured with much coarser curved striæ.

CARDIUM (PAPYRIDEA) BULLATUM, Chemnitz.

Hab. West Indies, Brazil, and west coast of Central America. St. Vincent, Cape Verde Islands (*Dunker*).

The synonymy of this species I have given in the Report of the

'Challenger' Lamellibranchiata, p. 161. It has not previously been met with so far south in the eastern parts of the Atlantic.

ROCELLARIA DUBIA (Pennant).

Hab. Mediterranean, Red Sea, North Sea, Madeira, Canary Islands, Cape Verde Islands.

St. Helena is, I believe, the most southern locality known for this species.

CHAMA, sp.

Several specimens of a species of this genus were collected by Capt. Turton. The young examples exhibit short spines on both valves, but the adult shells are too worn to be determined. The interior is white, more or less stained with brown, especially towards the margins. Length of largest specimen 75 millim.

C. gryphoides, Linn., appears in Jeffreys's and Melliss's lists of St. Helena shells. I have not seen the specimens which they examined, but doubtless they belonged to the same species as those collected by Capt. Turton. It is probable that they are correctly identified, but in such a difficult group as *Chama* one hesitates to pronounce a positive opinion without a special study.

BASTEROTIA OBLONGA.   (Plate XXII. figs. 5, 5 a.)

Testa oblongo-subquadrata, valde inæquilateralis, albida, concentrice striata; valvæ æquales, ab umbone ad extremitatem posticam obtuse angulatæ; margo dorsi posticus fere rectus, ventralis subrectilinearis, vel in medio leviter incurvatus; latus anticum breve, obliquum, inferne rotundatum, posticum oblique curvatum, ad extremitatem acute rotundatum; umbones parvi, acuti, antemediani, circiter in ⅓ longitudinis siti; dens cardinalis in utraque valva prominens, acutus; pagina interna nitida; cicatrices bene impressæ.

Longit. 8½ millim., *alt.* 5, *diam.* 4½.

This is a more oblong species than *B. carinata* or *B. gouldii* and some others.

This group of shells was first recognized by Gray in 1842 (Synopsis Contents Brit. Mus. p. 78) and named *Harlea*. His description runs thus:—"The *Harlea* are oblong, subquadrate, thin shells, with a sharp keel from the umbo, and conical hinge-teeth."

This diagnosis applies perfectly to the type marked by Gray himself as *Harlea*, and this was described the year following (1843) by Hinds as *Corbula quadrata*. This species also forms the type of Récluz's genus *Eucharis* (1850), and Hörnes in 1859 described a fossil species belonging to the same group under the generic name *Basterotia*. Considering the imperfection of Gray's description, and the fact of his not citing any species, I think it would be advisable to ignore his genus *Harlea*, although, personally, I am sure what group he intended to include under that name.

A genus *Eucharis* having been published by Latreille in 1804, this name cannot be employed for the present group of shells. We

21*

are therefore compelled to designate it *Basterotia*, the name given
by Hörnes, who appears to have been ignorant of the fact that, not
only Gray, but Récluz also, had previously recognized the existence
of this generic group.

LASÆA ADANSONIANA (Récluz).

Poronia adansoniana, Récluz, Rev. Zool. 1843, p. 174; id. in
Chenu's Illus. Conchyl. pl. i. figs. 1 a–g.

Hab. Senegal.

LUCINA INCONSPICUA. (Plate XXII. fig. 6.)

*Testa minima, altior quam longa, mediocriter convexa, inæqui-
laterialis, solidiuscula, albida, concentrice regulariter tenuiter
striata, striisque radiantibus vix conspicuis sculpta ; umbones
acuti, antrorsum curvati ; lunula profunda, parva ; margo
dorsi posticus leviter excurvatus ; pagina interna nitida,
ad marginem minute denticulata ; dentes cardinales et laterales
validi.*

Longit. 3 *millim.*, alt. 3⅓, diam. 2.

This species, although so small, is conspicuously solid. The umbones are well curved forward, producing a beaked appearance to the
apex. The radiating striæ are excessively fine and only visible in
certain lights, and seem to be lines below the surface.

LUCINA (CODAKIA) COMPACTA. (Plate XXII. fig. 7.)

*Testa æquilateralis, mediocriter globosa, alba vel dilute citrina,
concentrice et radiatim tenuissime et confertim lirata, minute
cancellata ; umbones leviter prominentes ; lunula angusta, parva,
mediocriter profunda ; latus posticum obtusum, anticum rotundatum ; margo inferior intus striatus, subcrenulatus ; ligamentum internum.*

Longit. 10 *millim.*, alt. 9½, diam. 6.

The dentition and the muscular impressions of this species are
normal. The sculpture is so fine that it is almost invisible to the
naked eye. Specimens were collected both by Capt. Turton and
Mr. Melliss. It appears to be a common species.

VERTICORDIA ORNATA (d'Orbigny).

The three odd valves from St. Helena agree precisely with those
described in my Report on the Lamellibranchiata of the 'Challenger'
Expedition, p. 166. The synonymy and distribution of this species
are there given. St. Helena is the most southern known locality.

MYTILUS EXUSTUS, Linn.

Mytilus exustus, Reeve, Conch. Icon. fig. 10; Clessin, Conch.-
Cab. ed. 2, pl. 16. figs. 7, 8.

Hab. West Indies, Brazil, U. States as far north as Charleston.

A few small odd valves, received in 1865 from the Museum of
Economic Geology, apparently belong to this species.

LITHODOMUS BI-EXCAVATUS, Reeve?

L. bi-excavatus, Reeve, Conch. Icon. pl. 4. figs. 22 *a*, *b*.

Hab. St. Thomas, West Indies.

The shells obtained at St. Helena by Mr. Melliss and named *L. lithophagus*, Linn., by Jeffreys, do not belong to that species. They may be considered a variety of *L. bi-excavatus*, in which the two depressions are not quite so distinct as in the type. The chalky incrustation which invests them has a more openly reticulated or spongy appearance at the posterior end.

ARCA SANCTÆ-HELENÆ.   (Plate XXII. figs. 8–8 *b*.)

Testa oblonga, crassa, albida, rufo-strigata et variegata, inferne haud hians ; valvæ solidæ, antice oblique curvatæ, postice paulo latiores, curvatim truncatæ, radiatim costatæ, lineisque tenui- bus concentricis et transversis decussatæ ; costæ inæquales, subnodosæ, anteriores et posteriores crassæ, medianæ tenuiores ; pagina interna alba, ad marginem saturate purpureo-fusca postice fortiter dentata ; umbones remoti, incurvati, prominentes ; liga- menti area lata, concava ; ligamentum subrhomboidale, fuscum, sulcis paucis sculptum.

Longit. 66 *millim.*, *diam.* 47, *alt.* 36.

This is a strong, heavy species, belonging to the same group as *A. noæ*, *A. navicularis*, and the like.

It is more solid than either of the above-named species, has the posterior end unsinuated, and the margins of the valves are peculiarly dentate posteriorly, and, when closed, interlock like the valves of *Ostrea crista-galli* and some others.   A few of the ribs near the posterior angle of the valves are very large and strong, and separated by very deep grooves.

The form is rather like that of *A. subquadrangula* of Dunker, but the posterior end is not so truncate and the costæ are different.

ARCA (ACAR) DOMINGENSIS, Lamarck.

Hab. West Indies, Cape Verde Islands, S. Africa, Red Sea, Indian Ocean, South Pacific Ocean, Japan, Australia, &c. (*Lischke*).

PINNA RUGOSA, Sowerby.

Pinna rugosa, Sowerby, Reeve, Conch. Icon. pl. 26. fig. 50.

Hab. Isle of Rey, Bay of Panama (*Cuming*).

Capt. Turton remarks as follows respecting the single broken valve obtained :—" It measured when perfect 19 inches, but I cannot be sure of this identical shell being an island one, as I bought it ; but I have seen another just like it, 16 inches long, which was fished up alive and bought by another officer before I heard of it, so this is probably an island one too."

Is there some mistake here, or does this species really occur at Panama?

PINNA PERNULA, Chemnitz.

Pinna pernula, Chemn., Reeve, Conch. Icon. pl. 12. figs. 22 *a*, *b*.
Hab. St. Croix, West Indies (*Chemnitz*) ; Madeira (*Brit. Mus.*).

AVICULA HIRUNDO (Linn.).
Hab. On the sea-beach, St. Helena (*Melliss*).

PECTEN CORALLINOIDES, d'Orbigny.

Pecten corallinoides, d'Orb. in Webb & Berthelot's Hist. Nat.
Canaries, Mollusques, p. 102, pl. 7*b*. figs. 20–22 ; Sowerby, Thes.
Conch. vol. ii. p. 65, pl. 12. figs. 3, 4.

Hab. Canary Islands, Cape Verde Islands.

This striking species has not previously been recorded from so
southern a locality.

PECTEN ATLANTICUS.   (Plate XXII. figs. 9–9 *b*.)

*Testa obliqua, inæquilateralis, æquivalvis, mediocriter convexa,
albida vel flavescens,supra costas rufo vel roseo tincta et maculata,
costis rotundatis circiter 16, sulcos immaculatos modice profundos
æquantibus, instructa, inter et supra costas liris tenuibus, minute
squamosis, ornata ; auriculæ parvæ, inæquales, postica valvæ
dextræ oblique declivis, liris tenuibus radiantibus 5–7 instructa,
antica paulo major, radiatim lirata, minute squamosa, inferne
vix sinuata ; auriculæ valvæ sinistræ liris tenuibus, paucis,
squamatis, ornatæ ; pagina interna flavo-albida, plus minus
rubicunda.*

Longit. 29 *millim.*, *diam.* 15, *alt.* 29.

This species is remarkable on account of its oblique form, which
is produced by the posterior slope being longer than the anterior.
The angle at the apex, formed by the dorsal slopes, is about equal
to a right angle. The surface is rough to the touch through the
beautiful wavy lines of growth which everywhere adorn the surface,
and, upon the ridges, become minute scales.

PECTEN (JANIRA) TURTONI.   (Plate XXII. figs. 10, 10 *a*.)

*Testa rotundata ; valva plana leviter concava, rufescens vel
rosacea, maculis albis, lineisque gracilibus, zigzagformibus,
purpureis, ornata, costis radiantibus, tenuibus, aurantio-rufis,
circiter 17–19, instructa, lineis incrementi confertis, elevatis,
pulcherrime lamellata ; valva convexa, mediocriter profunda
vel purpurea, apicem versus pallida vel albida, inter costas
purpureo tincta, costis paulo latioribus et planioribus quam in
valva superiore ; auriculæ parvæ, plus minus purpureo tinctæ ;
pagina interna valvæ profundæ alba, fusco-purpureo marginata,
v. planæ in medio aurantio vel roseo, et ad marginem purpureo
tincta.*

Longit. et latit. 32–34 *millim.*

The fine ribs, the comparatively small auricles, and the beautiful
raised lamelliform lines of growth are the chief distinguishing

features of this species. It probably attains larger dimensions than those given above. The angle formed by the divergent dorsal slopes is about 116 degrees.

LIMEA SARSII, Lovén.

Limea sarsii, Lovén, Index Moll. Scandin. p. 32.

Lima sarsii, Jeffreys, Brit. Conch. vol. ii. p. 78, vol. v. p. 169, pl. 25. fig. 1.

Lima (Limatula) sarsii, Jeffreys, Proc. Zool. Soc. 1879, p. 562.

Limatula crassa (Forbes), Sars, Moll. Reg. Arct. Norv. p. 26.

Hab. North Sea; Mediterranean; Atlantic from west of Ireland to Portugal.

A number of odd valves were dredged in deep water by Capt. Turton. The occurrence of this species so far south has not been previously noted.

OSTREA, sp.

A species of oyster occurs in very shallow pools on the east coast of St. Helena, which, possibly, has not been previously described. The same form is met with at Cape Verde Islands. It is thick, solid, irregularly rounded, with the surface ridged and the margin dentate and interlocking like *O. folium* and other species. The interior is dirty whitish, stained more or less with olive-brown or yellowish olive, and the outer margin is finely wrinkle-striated.

OSTREA CRISTA-GALLI, Linn.

Hab. St. Helena, 50–60 fathoms (*Melliss*).

I have not seen the specimens collected by Mr. Melliss and identified by Jeffreys as belonging to this species, which is usually regarded as an Indian-Ocean form. I think it probable that they belong to the same species as those collected by Capt. Turton, which I have not ventured to identify. Having strongly dentate margins to the valves, they may have been mistaken by Jeffreys for the Linnean species.

APPENDIX.

The following species were all taken at St. Helena upon floating seaweed, but, as I have already shown [1], are to be regarded as South-African forms.

I. GASTROPODA.

PLEUROTOMA (MANGILIA) ATLANTICA. (Plate XXIV. fig. 11.)

Testa elongata, pallide fusca, linea alba cincta ; anfractus 5, primus maximus, globosus, nitidus, albidus, cæteri convexiusculi, plicis longitudinalibus 10–12 instructi, liris striisque spiralibus ornati ; anfr. ultimus elongatus, infra medium parum contractus ; apertura angusta, longit. totius 7/12 adæquans ; columella alba ; labrum vix incrassatum, superne minime sinuatum.

Longit. 6 millim., *diam. max.* 2¼.

This species is remarkable for the large size of the apex. The

[1] Pp. 247, 248.

general colour of the shell appears to be brown or reddish, but on close examination it will be seen that the spiral striæ are whitish, and the interstices or liræ only are coloured.

PLEUROTOMA (MANGILIA) CASTA, Reeve.

The single shell collected by Capt. Turton agrees in many respects with the type of this species, which, unfortunately, is in rather bad condition, and only exhibits faint indications of spiral striæ. The specimen from the "Sea-horn" is beautifully striated, is rather shorter, and has one costa less than the type. Nevertheless, I have a strong belief that it belongs to the same species. The locality of *P. casta* was unknown to Reeve.

MUREX (OCINEBRA) PURPUROIDES, Dunker.

Hab. Cape of Good Hope.

COLUMBELLA (ANACHIS) KRAUSSII, Sowerby.

Columbella kraussii, Sowerby (1844), Thesaurus, Conch. vol. ii. p. 144, pl. xl. figs. 180, 181 ; Reeve, Conch. Icon. fig. 213.

Buccinum cereale (Menke, MS.), Krauss (1848), Südafr. Moll. p. 122, pl. vi. fig. 17 ; Reeve, Conch. Icon. (*Columbella*), pl. xxi. fig. 118.

Columbella (Anachis) fulminea, Gould, Proc. Bost. Soc. Nat. Hist. vol. vii. p. 334 ; Otia, p. 131.

This seems to be rather a common shell on the South-African coast. *C. fulminea* was described from Simon's Bay, Krauss cites the Cape Coast for it, and in the Museum there is a series labelled Natal. Two specimens only, of a rather dark tint, were obtained at St. Helena.

COLUMBELLA (MITRELLA) PROSCRIPTA.   (Plate XXIV. fig. 12.)

Testa minuta, angusta, tenuis, nitida, pallide fuscescens, infra suturam linea saturatiore cincta, versus apicem dilute rosacea; anfractus 5, primi duo magni, læves, convexi, cæteri convexiusculi, striis paucis spiralibus pallidis (in anfr. ultimo circiter 12) sculpti; apertura angusta, longit. totius ⅓ vix æquans; labrum leviter incrassatum, superne subsinuatum, ad marginem fusco tinctum; columella rectiuscula, callo tenui induta.

Longit. 4 millim., diam. 1½.

A small shining pinkish-brown shell, exhibiting a few spiral pale striæ. The penultimate and antepenultimate volutions show indications of longitudinal plication.

PURPURA SQUAMOSA, Lamarck.

Hab. Cape of Good Hope and Natal coast (*Krauss* and others); St. Vincent, Cape Verde Islands (*Dunker*).

Only one young specimen of this common South-African species was sent by Capt. Turton. The locality given by Reeve (Con. Icon. sp. 48), "Tigre Bay, Abyssinia," requires confirmation. It may be correct, but the number of species common to South Africa and the Red Sea is not large.

MARGINELLA (VOLVARIA) ZONATA, Kiener.

The single specimen from St. Helena is small, about the same size as the form described by Krauss (Südafr. Moll. p. 126) under the name *M. dunkeri*, but the labrum at the upper extremity is united with the shell *at* the suture and *not below* it. The position of this point of juncture, judging from the series of specimens in the Museum, is variable, and consequently when it is high up at the suture the upper margin of the brownish-yellow band will fall further below than when the end of the labrum is attached further down or below the suture. I am therefore of opinion that *M. dunkeri* should be regarded as a variety of *M. zonata* and not as a distinct species, as the distinctive features referred to by Krauss are not constant.

Weinkauff (Monograph of *Marginella*, Conch.-Cab. ed. 2, p. 28) quotes this species as *M. dunkeri* from Ascension Island, his specimens being almost as large as typical examples of *M. zonata*, which appear to be common at the Cape of Good Hope.

MITRA SIMPLEX, Dunker.

Hab. Cape of Good Hope.

RISSOA PLATIA.   (Plate XXIV. fig. 13.)

Testa minuta, ovato-turrita, imperforata, albida; anfractus 4½, superne concave excavati, in medio subacute angulati, infra angulum contracti, spiraliter lirati; apex obtusus, involutus; apertura rotunde ovata, superne acuminata, longit. totius ⅓ subæquans; peristoma continuum, incrassatum, subeffusum, margine columellari inferne subproducta.

Longit. 1⅔ *millim., diam.* ⅔.

The spiral sculpture is continued upon the apical whorl, which is involuted, thus producing a very blunt top to the shell. The liræ are four to six in number on the lower half of the penultimate whorl, and rather coarser than those above the angle.

RISSOA ATOMUS.   (Plate XXIV. fig. 14.)

Testa minuta, alba, pellucida, nitida, ovata, imperforata; anfractus 4, convexiusculi, læves, ultimus magnus; apertura subpyriformis, longit. totius ⅔ adæquans; peristoma continuum, margine externo leviter patulo et incrassato, columellari obliquo, superne valde calloso.

Longit. 1 *millim., diam.* ½.

This minute species, of which there are three specimens, is certainly full-grown, and has no other sculpture except microscopic lines of growth.

RISSOA VAGA.   (Plate XXIV. fig. 15.)

Testa minuta, tenuis, subrimata, dilute fuscescens, spiraliter lirata; anfractus 5, convexi, liris filiformibus spiralibus (in anfr. penult. 3, ultimo 10) instructi; apertura ovato-rotundata, longit. totius

⅓ *subæquans; peristoma tenue, margine columellari leviter reflexo, superne labro callo tenui juncto.*

Longit. 2 *millim., diam.* 1.

This species has more convex whorls than *R. varicifera*, to which it bears a general resemblance. Its spiral ridges also are finer, the aperture different, and the labrum has no external varix.

Rissoa simulans.   (Plate XXIV. fig. 16.)

Testa ovata, imperforata, alba vel pallide fuscescens; anfractus 4, convexi, primus et secundus spiraliter striati, sequentes liris transversis (in anfr. penultimo circiter 3, in ultimo 8–9) instructi; apertura rotunde ovata, longit. totius ½ paulo minor; peristoma continuum, vix incrassatum, margine columellari anguste reflexo.

Longit. 1⅔ *millim., diam.* 1.

This is a shorter stumpier species than *R. varicifera* and has no postlabral thickening.

Rissoa ordinaria.   (Plate XXIV. fig. 17.)

Testa ovata, solidiuscula, alba, imperforata, nitida; anfractus 4, convexiusculi, sutura mediocriter profunda, paulo obliqua sejuncti, spiraliter substriati; apertura rotunde ovata, superne acuminata, longit. totius ½ paulo superans; peristoma continuum, leviter incrassatum, margine columellari dilatato.

Longit. 1⅓ *millim., diam.* ⅔.

This species, although so small, is certainly adult. The spiral striæ are not numerous, and only visible on well-preserved specimens by the aid of a microscope.

Rissoa æqua.   (Plate XXIV. fig. 18.)

Testa brevis, turrita, alba, vix rimata; anfractus 5, primi duo convexi, læves vel spiraliter tenuiter striati, cæteri superne tabulati, angulati, carinis fortibus (in anfr. superioribus duabus, in ultimo senis) instructi, lineis incrementi tenuissimis sculpti; apertura ovata, longit. totius ½ haud æquans; peristoma continuum, margine externo vix incrassato, columellari dilatato, reflexo, rimam umbilicalem formante.

Longit. 2½ *millim., diam.* 1½.

This species closely resembles *R. perfecta* in form. It is, however, a little larger, is not spotted, and has seven keels on the body-whorl instead of five; of these, the one nearest the suture is very fine and thread-like, the next two, which also pass up the spire, are strong and prominent, and the remaining four gradually lessen in thickness, the lowermost being very inconspicuous.

The nucleus of this species is also different from that of *R. perfecta*, and the outer lip is not thickened in the same manner.

Rissoa fenestrata, Krauss.

Hab. Cape of Good Hope.

BARLEEIA WALLICHI. (Plate XXIV. fig. 19.)

Testa B. congenitœ *similis, sed tenuior, pallidior, spiraliter tenuissime striata ; anfractus 5, conveviusculi, ultimus rotundatus, haud obsolete angulatus ; peristoma undique tenue, marginibus callo tenui junctis.*

Longit. 2 millim., diam. 1.

This species in form is very like *B. congenita,* from St. Helena. It is, however, rather smaller, thinner, paler, spirally striated, has no approach to an angle at the periphery, and has a thinner peristome.

TURRITELLA CARINIFERA, Lamarck.

Hab. Cape of Good Hope.

TRIFORIS PERVERSA (Linné).

Hab. South Africa (*G. B. Sowerby*).

This well-known species occurs in Great Britain, Mediterranean, at Madeira and the Canary Islands, also on the coast of California.

TURBO (OCANA) CIDARIS, Gmelin.

Hab. Cape of Good Hope.

TURBO (COLLONIA) INCERTUS. (Plate XXIV. figs. 21, 21 *a.*)

Testa minuta, imperforata, subglobosa, fusco-purpurea, lœvis, incrementi lineis striata ; anfractus tres, conveviusculi, celeriter crescentes, ultimus magnus, rotundatus ; apertura magna, fere circularis, longit. totius ⅔ fere œquans ; peristoma interruptum, margine exteriori tenui, columellari albo, incrassato, reflexo.

Longit. 1⅓ *millim., diam. maj.* 1⅘.

The generic position of this minute species, of which there are five specimens in the collection, would be somewhat uncertain, if the operculum had not been present in one of the examples. It is white, slightly convex, and consists of about three whorls.

PHASIANELLA NERITINA, Dunker.

Hab. Cape of Good Hope.

TROCHUS (CYNISCA) GRANULOSUS, Dunker.

Hab. Table Bay, Cape of Good Hope.

The type figured by Krauss (Südafr. Moll. pl. v. fig. 28) is of a pinkish tint. White varieties are also met with. A. Adams described this species (P. Z. S. 1853, p. 183) as *Cyclostrema granulata.* The locality he gave, Philippine Islands, can scarcely be relied on.

TROCHUS (GIBBULA) MUSIVUS, Gould.

Hab. Simon's Bay, Cape of Good Hope (*Gould*).

SCISSURELLA JUCUNDA. (Plate XXIV. figs. 22, 22 *a.*)

Testa minuta, umbilicata, depressa, alba; anfractus tres, convexi, liris spiralibus, tenuissimis, aliisque radiantibus, cancellati, ultimus

liris duobus elevatis fissuram contingentibus superne instructus ;
apertura irregulariter rotundata ; peristoma tenue, continuum.
Diam. maj. 1¼ millim.

There are two specimens of this very minute shell. The larger
has the slit almost closed at the peristome, which is otherwise continuous, so that it is likely, if it had lived a short time longer, it
would have been quite closed, and then would have become a form
of *Schismope.*

In his report on the Gasteropoda of the 'Challenger' Expedition,
p. 119, Mr. Watson has described as *Schismope carinata* the same
species as that published by A. Adams (Ann. Mag. Nat. Hist. 1862,
vol. x. p. 346) under the name of *Scissurella carinata.*

FISSURELLA MUTABILIS, Sowerby.

Hab. South Africa, at the Cape.

PATELLA UMBELLA, Gmelin.

Hab. South Africa, Cape of Good Hope.

PATELLA RUSTICA, Linn.

Hab. South Africa, Cape of Good Hope.

PATELLA OCULUS, Born.

Hab. Cape of Good Hope.

PATELLA COMPRESSA, Linné.

The two specimens from St. Helena are of an unusual bright red
colour, and the interior, excepting the muscular scar and the part it
encloses, is of the same bright colour. They are in an excellent
state of preservation, exhibiting on and between the fine radiating
liræ very pretty close-set concentric wavy striæ.

Although found on the beach by Capt. Turton, these specimens
have doubtless been transported from the Cape of Good Hope to
St. Helena upon floating seaweed, upon the stems of which it is said
to attach itself.

CYLICHNA REMISSA. (Plate XXIV. fig. 20.)

Testa parva, tenuis, albida, superne anguste perforata, striis spira-
libus et longitudinalibus minute decussata ; anfr. ultimus lateribus
rectiusculis, inferne paulo latior quam supra ; apertura supra
angusta, infra medium leviter dilatata ; columella obliqua,
subrecta, leviter reflexa.
Longit. 2¼ millim., diam. 1¼.

This species has much resemblance to *Utriculus complanatus,*
Watson, in form. It is, however, a little narrower at the upper
part, and the aperture is produced higher above the spire. The
reticulate sculpture can only be seen under a compound microscope.

II. PELECYPODA.

SAXICAVA ARCTICA (Linn.).

Hab. Cosmopolitan.

KELLIA CRASSIUSCULA.   (Plate XXIV. fig. 23.)

Testa globosa, rotunde ovata, nitida, alba, apices versus subpellucida, concentrice subrugose striata, fere æquilateralis ; latus anticum posteriore paulo angustius ; pagina interna alba, incrassata, minute subrugosa ; linea cardinalis crassiuscula, dente vel tuber- culo cardinali et laterali posteriore tuberculari in utraque valva instructa ; ligamentum internum pone umbones situm.

Longit. 6¼ *millim., alt.* 5, *diam.* 3¾.

For a shell of such small size it is rather thick. The umboues are only very slightly elevated, curved towards the anterior end, and capped at the tip with a minute embryonic shell.

KELLIA ATLANTICA.   (Plate XXIV. fig. 24.)

Testa minuta, oblongo-rotundata, inæquilateralis, sordide albida, concentrice tenuissime striata ; margo dorsi anticus valde declivis, leviter convexus, posticus longior, subhorizontalis ; latus anticum acute rotundatum, posticum latius excurvatum ; margo inferior late arcuatus. Dens cardinalis valvæ sinistræ ∧·formæ, valvæ dextræ unicus prominens, acutus ; dens lateralis posticus in utraque valva elongatus, in dextra validus, margine dorsali sulco separatus.

Longit. 2½ *millim., alt.* 2, *diam.* 1⅓.

This species is about the size of *Lepton clarkiæ,* but not of the same form.

MONTACUTA SUBTRIANGULARIS.   (Plate XXIV. fig. 25.)

Testa fere æquilateralis, mediocriter convexa, sordide albida, haud nitida, rotunde subtriangularis, lineis incrementi striata, postice quam antice paulo angustior ; margo dorsalis utrinque declivis, postice vix excurvatus, antice leviter concavus, ventralis rectus vel in medio levissime incurvatus ; umbones prominuli, subacuti ; pagina interna nitida, prope margine incrassata ; cicatrices magnæ, subpyriformes ; dentes duo valvæ sinistræ prominentes, divergentes.

Longit. 4½ *millim., alt.* 3⅓, *diam.* 2½.

This species has the dorsal margin sloping on each side and the base almost straight, so that a somewhat triangular shape is produced, the two lower angles being well rounded.

LUCINA (CODAKIA) IMBRICATULA, C. B. Adams.

Lucina imbricatula, C. B. Adams, Proc. Boston Soc. Nat. Hist. 1845, vol. ii. p. 10 ; id. Contrib. Conch. p. 245.

Lucina pecten, Reeve (non Lamarck), Conch. Icon. pl. 7. figs. 34, 35 *a–b*.

Lucina occidentalis, Reeve, Conch. Icon. Index, Errata.

Hab. Various islands in the West Indies, also Cape Verde Islands (*P. Furse* in Brit. Mus.).

This species greatly resembles *L. fibula* Reeve, from the Philippines, Red Sea, &c., but the radiating ridges do not divaricate on the dorsal margins in the same manner. *L. munda*, A. Adams (Proc. Zool. Soc. 1855, p. 225), is the same species as *L. fibula*.

MYTILUS EDULIS, Linné?

Two or three small specimens collected by Mr. Melliss have been referred to this common species by Jeffreys. They were " found attached to long pieces of seaweed " which drift on shore at Sandy Bay beach on the south coast (Melliss), so probably had been carried northward from S. Africa. They might with equal propriety be referred to *M. compressus*, Phil., or *M. meridionalis*, Krauss.

MYTILUS MAGELLANICUS, Chemnitz.

Both Mr. Melliss and Capt. Turton obtained this form from seaweed. The specimens are all small, about an inch in length, and show considerable variation in the number and coarseness of the ribs. The colour varies from yellow to purplish.

MODIOLARIA MARMORATA (Forbes).

Hab. Gt. Britain, Mediterranean, Canary Islands.

According to Jeffreys this species also occurs in the Gulf of Suez, the Persian Gulf, and N. Pacific. The specimens from St. Helena collected by Capt. Turton are vividly mottled, but agree in form and sculpture with European specimens.

CRENELLA PURA.   (Plate XXIV. fig. 26.)

Testa minuta, æquilateralis, triangularis, inferne arcuata, alba ; valvæ mediocriter convexæ, crassiusculæ, radiatim anguste sulcata, sulcis interstitiis angustioribus, lineis incrementi striata ; margo dorsi utrinque valde declivis, subrectilinearis ; umbones prominentes ; linea cardinis valida, infra et pone umbones transversim striata, sulco angusto ligamentali postice obliquo sculpta ; pagina interna nitida, alba, haud margaritacea, margine inferiori plus minus denticulato, dentibus 2–3 validis ad extremitatem posticam lineæ cardinalis instructa.

Longit. 3 millim., alt. 3⅓, diam. 2.

This little species for its size is rather solid, and peculiar on account of its hinge-plate, and the two or three denticles at the posterior end, just within the margin of the valves.

PECTEN PUSIO, Linn.

Hab. Mediterranean to Norway and Faroe Isles, Madeira, Canaries, Azores, S. Africa.

This species has been quoted from South Africa both by Jeffreys

and Sowerby.   The latter has, correctly I think, cited *P. tinctus* and
P. albus of Reeve as synonyms.   In this category I should also place
P. sentis and *P. textilis* of the same author.

EXPLANATION OF THE PLATES.
PLATE XXI.

Fig. 1. *Pleurotoma (Clavus) amanda*, p. 255.
   2. —— (——) *albobalteata*, p. 255.
   3. —— (*Drillia*) *turtoni*, p. 256.
   4. —— (*Mangilia*) *subquadrata*, p. 256.
   5. —— (——) *mellissi*, p. 257.
   6. —— (*Clathurella?*) *multigranosa*, p. 258.
   7. *Murex (Ocinebra) alboangulatus*, p. 259.
   8. *Lachesis helenæ*, p. 260.
   9. *Cantharus (Tritonidea) albozonatus*, p. 260.
  10. —— (——) *consanguineus*, p. 260.
  11. —— (——) *lævis*, p. 261.
  12. *Columbella (Mitrella) sanctæ-helenæ*, p. 262.
  13. *Triton turtoni*, p. 268.
13 *a*. —— —— ; young.
  14. *Natica turtoni*, p. 269.
14 *a*. —— —— ; operculum, p. 270.
  15. —— *tæniata*; operculum, p. 270.
  16. —— *sanctæ-helenæ*, p. 270.
  17. *Solarium ordinarium*; upper side, p. 281.
17 *a*. —— —— ; front view.
17 *b*. —— —— ; lower side.
  18. *Eulima (Subularia) fuscopunctata*, p. 280.
  19. *Littorina helenæ*, p. 283.
  20. *Diala fuscopicta*, p. 286.
  21. *Rissoa cala*, p. 288.
  22. —— *ephamilla*, p. 288.
  23. —— *agapeta*, p. 289.
  24. —— *wallichi*, p. 289.
  25. *Barleeia congenita*, p. 290.
  26. *Triforis atlantica*, p. 292.

PLATE XXII.

Fig. 1. *Mitra (Cancilla) turtoni*, p. 265.
   2. —— (*Pusia*) *sanctæ-helenæ*, p. 265.
   3. *Obeliscus (Syrnola) pumilio*, p. 275.
   4. *Turbo (Collonia) admissus*, p. 294.
   5. *Basterotia oblonga*; lateral view, p. 303.
5 *a*. —— —— ; dorsal side.
   6. *Lucina inconspicua*, p. 304.
   7. —— (*Codakia*) *compacta*, p. 304.
   8. *Arca sanctæ-helenæ*; lateral view, p. 305.
8 *a*. —— —— ; dorsal side.
8 *b*. —— —— ; ventral side.
   9. *Pecten atlanticus*, p. 306.
9 *a*. —— —— ; sculpture magnified.
9 *b*. —— —— ; sculpture of left valve.
  10. —— (*Janira*) *turtoni*; right valve, p. 306.
10 *a*. —— (——) —— ; left valve.

PLATE XXIII.

Fig. 1. *Pleurotoma (Clavus) prolongata*, p. 255.
   2. —— (*Mangilia*) *gemma*, p. 256.
   3. —— (*Clathurella?*) *commutabilis*, p. 257.
   4. —— (——) *usta*, p. 258.

Fig. 20. *Cylichna remissa*, p. 312.
 21. *Turbo* (*Collinia*) *incertus*, p. 311.
 21 *a*. ——— (———) ——— ; upper view.
 22. *Scissurella jucunda*, p. 311.
 22 *a*. ——— ——— ; upper surface.
 23. *Kellia crassiuscula*, p. 313.
 24. ——— *atlantica*, p. 313.
 25. *Montacuta subtriangularis*, p. 313.
 26. *Crenella pura*, p. 314.

4. On the Marine Mollusca of Ascension Island.
By Edgar A. Smith.

[Received March 14, 1890.]

In the following list of forty-two species of Mollusca from Ascension Island, nine, obtained by the 'Challenger' Expedition, ought not perhaps to be included in the fauna; for, although dredged close to the island off the west coast, they were from a depth of 420 fathoms.

The poverty of this list is doubtless due to the fact that no experienced collector has ever explored the shores.

Fourteen of these species occur at St. Helena, eleven are West-African, twelve are found at the Cape Verde, Canary Islands, and the Azores, nine are Mediterranean, and seventeen, or about 40 per cent., are West-Indian forms. These figures, on comparison with those referring to the species found at St. Helena, and given in the previous report, show that the relationship of the two faunas to other regions is the same. Both resemble that of the West Indies more than any other locality, both have a considerable percentage of species common to West Africa, to the Atlantic Islands, including the Cape Verdes, Canaries, Madeira, and the Azores, and also to the Mediterranean, the causes which have effected this distribution doubtless being the same in both cases.

The three species of *Marginella* are well-known Cape forms, and therefore the question arises, whether these shells may not have drifted to Ascension on floating tangles as in the case of numerous species at St. Helena.

A few species are eastern forms, for example *Ostrea cucullata* and *Malleus regula*. Both of these, I believe, are established at Ascension. The former was quoted by Chemnitz more than a hundred years ago, and although he remarks that ships returning from China and the East Indies used to call at Ascension for water, I do not think it likely that the shells were carried there from the east. The single valve received from Dr. Conry is in very fresh condition and has not the appearance of having been rolled on the beach.

In the 'Universal Conchologist' Martyn has figured a small specimen of the well-known *Fusus proboscidiferus* of Lamarck, under the name of *Buccinum incisum*, and gives as the locality "Ascension Island, new Guinea."